CRANK PALACE

A MAZE RUNNER NOVELLA

#1 NY TIMES BEST-SELLING AUTHOR

JAMES DASHNER

For more information contact:
Riverdale Avenue Books/Quest Imprint
5676 Riverdale Avenue
Riverdale, NY 10471

www.riverdaleavebooks.com

Design by www.formatting4U.com
Cover design by Scott Carpenter

Digital ISBN: 9781626015661
Trade ISBN: 9781626015678
Hardcover ISBN: 9781626015685

First edition, November 2020

Dedication

To Lynette,
my loving wife, my hilarious best friend,
my adventure partner,
who has always been my first reader
and biggest supporter.

To our children,
Wesley, Bryson, Kayla, and Dallin,
the final pieces of the puzzle,
who've continually inspired me
and kept me on track with life.

To Tomoya,
my son Wesley's (and now our family) friend,
who provided the spark for the character of Keisha.

Finally, to my readers,
who show me each and every day
how to fight for a better future.

Author's Note

I've always been fascinated by viruses and plagues. What does that say about me? Not sure. But our world history is chock-full of devastating periods of illness and disease that wiped out huge proportions of the population. There are many scary things in life, many things that can kill you, but for me personally, dying from a microscopic invader that you can't see coming... well, that's some serious terror right there.

It should come as no surprise, then, that the Flare virus was a central element of *The Maze Runner* series. I was fully aware that such a plot point had been done ad nauseam, in many variations, in books and movies and television shows before I wrote about it. That didn't faze me. I wanted terror as a backdrop, and so I chose my most terrifying thing, with a twist. A virus that attacks your brain, drives you slowly insane, takes away every aspect of your humanity, until you're a raging, mindless beast.

Happy stuff, I know!

And now we have a virus of our own raging *its* way across the world. Covid-19 is no Flare, but it has brought just as much fear and suffering to those afflicted by its reach. And as of this writing, it's nowhere close to being contained. Scary. Heart-wrenching. Hopefully conquered sooner than later by humans pulling together to defeat it.

The reason I mention it is because a large chunk of *Crank Palace* was written after the latest coronavirus began its mad spread across continents, seemingly sparing no corner of the Earth, no matter how far. That was an odd experience. It added depth, a level of personal, relatable fear that might've been missing in earlier books. Most of all, I know it's affected many of my readers out there.

Two thousand and twenty has also brought to the forefront many of the others struggles you face. And I just want you to know that I care for you, deeply, that my gratitude for your support and love of this series is beyond my ability to craft words. And many things are in development to show you in a more tangible way just how much gratitude I've felt over these last years and months, as well as a desire to listen and learn from you.

This novella is something I'd been planning for a while, but it really gained steam over the last year or so. It's about Newt, during a period of *The Death Cure* in which we don't really know what happened to him. Certainly not what was going on inside his head. Well, you're about to find out. It will be a bittersweet journey, I'm sure.

This one is for you. All of my proceeds, from every version, every language, etc., will be going to charitable causes chosen by my followers on social media. It's the first, small way I can begin to say thank you, delivered in a neat little package, where you can live and celebrate and mourn with Newt one last time. I hope you enjoy the read.

Part One
Welcome to the Neighborhood

Chapter One

There they go.

Newt looked through the grimy glass of the Berg's porthole, watching as his friends walked toward the massive, imposing gate that barred one of the few passages into Denver. A formidable wall of cement and steel surrounded the city's battered-but-not-broken skyscrapers, with only a few checkpoints such as the one Newt's friends were about to use. *Attempt* to use. Looking up at the gray walls and the iron-colored bolts and seams and hinges of the reinforcements on the doors, it would be impossible not to think of the Maze, where the madness had all begun. Quite literally.

His friends.

Thomas.

Minho.

Brenda.

Jorge.

Newt had felt a lot of pain in his life, both inside and out, but he believed that very moment, watching Tommy and the others leave him for the last time, was his new rock bottom. He closed his eyes, the sorrow bearing on his heart like the weight of ten Grievers. Tears leaked out of his squeezed eyelids, ran down his face. His breath came in short, stuttered gasps. His chest hurt with the pain of it. A part of him desperately wanted to change his mind, accept the reckless whims of love and friendship and open the Berg's slanting hatch door, sprint down its rickety frame, join his friends in their quest to find Hans, get their implants removed, and accept whatever came next.

But he'd made up his mind, as fragile as it might be. If ever in his life he could do one thing right, the thing that was unselfish and full of good, this was it. He'd spare the people of Denver his disease, and he'd spare his friends the agony of watching him succumb to it.

His disease.

The Flare.

He hated it. He hated the people trying to find a cure. He hated that he wasn't immune and he hated that his best friends were. All of it conflicted, battled, raged inside him. He knew that he was slowly going insane, a fate rarely escaped when it came to the virus. It had come to a point where he didn't know if he could trust himself, both his thoughts and his feelings. Such an awful circumstance could drive a person mad if they weren't already well on their way to that lonely destination. But while he knew that he still had an ounce of sense, he needed to act. He needed to move, before all those heavy thoughts ended him even sooner than the Flare.

He opened his eyes, wiped his tears.

Tommy and the others had already made it through the checkpoint—they'd entered the testing area, anyway. What happened after that was cut from Newt's view with the closing of a gate, the final puncture in his withering heart. He turned his back to the window, pulled in several deep breaths, trying to dampen the anxiety that threatened him like a 30-meter wave.

I can do this, he thought. *For them.*

He got to his feet, ran to the bunk he'd used on the flight from Alaska. He had almost no possessions in this world, but what little he owned he threw into a backpack, including some water and food and a knife he'd stolen from Thomas to remember him by. Then he grabbed the most important item—a journal and pen he'd found in one of the random cabinets on the Berg. It had been blank when he'd discovered the compact book, though a little tattered and worn, its endless white pages flipping by like the rattled wings of a bird when he thumbed through it. Some former lost soul, flying to who knows where on this bucket of metal, had once thought to write down the story of their life but chickened out. Or died. Newt had decided on the spot to write his *own* story, keep it a secret from everyone else. For himself. Maybe someday for others.

The long blast of a horn sounded from outside the walls of the ship, making Newt flinch and throw himself onto the bed. His heart sputtered out a few rapid beats while he tried to reorient. The Flare made him jumpy, made him quick to anger, made him a sodden mess in every way. And it was only going to get worse—in fact, it seemed like the bloody thing was working overtime on his poor little brain. Stupid virus. He wished it was a person so he could kick its arse.

The noise stopped after a few seconds, followed by a silence still as darkness. Only in that silence did Newt realize that before the horn there'd been the ambient noise of people outside, erratic and... off. Cranks. They must be everywhere outside the walls of the city, those past the Gone, trying to get inside for no other reason than the madness that told them to do it. Desperate for food, like the primal animals they'd become.

What *he* would become.

But he had a plan, didn't he? Several plans, depending on the contingencies. But each plan had the same ending—it was just a matter of how he got there. He would last for as long as he needed to *write* what he needed in that journal. Something about that simple, empty little book, waiting to be filled. It had given him a purpose, a spark, a winding course to ensure the last days of his life had reason and meaning. A mark, left on the world. He would write all the sanity he could muster out of his head before it was taken over by its opposite.

He didn't know what the horn had been or who had blown it or why it was suddenly quiet outside. He didn't want to know. But perhaps a path had been cleared for him. The only item left to settle was how to leave it with Thomas and the others. Maybe give them a little closure. He'd already written one depressing note to Tommy; might as well write another.

Newt decided that his journal would survive if it weighed less by one page. He tore it out and sat down to write a message. Pen was almost to paper when he stalled, as if he'd had the perfect thing to say but it floated out of his mind like vanished smoke. Sighing, he itched with irritation. Anxious to get out of that Berg, walk away—limp or no limp—before something changed, he scribbled down a few lines, the first things that popped in his head.

They got inside somehow. They're taking me to live with the other Cranks.

It's for the best. Thanks for being my friends.

Goodbye.

It wasn't totally true, but he thought about those horns and all that commotion he'd heard outside the Berg and figured it was close. Was it short and curt enough to prevent them from coming after him? To get it through their thick skulls that there was no hope for him and that he'd only get in the way? That he didn't want them to watch him turn into a mad, raving, cannibalistic former human?

Didn't matter. Didn't matter at all. He was going one way or another.

To give his friends the best shot they had at succeeding, with one less obstacle.

One less Newt.

Chapter Two

The streets were chaos, a mass of disorder shaken up like dice and spilled across the land.

But that wasn't the scary part. The scary part was how *normal* everything felt—as if the world had been arcing toward this moment since the day its rocky surface first cooled and the oceans ceased to boil. Remnants of suburbs lay in scattered, trashy ruin; buildings and homes with broken windows and peeled paint; garbage everywhere, strewn about like the tattered pieces of a shattered sky; crumpled, filthy, fire-scorched vehicles of all sorts; vegetation and trees growing in places never meant for them. And worst of all, Cranks ambling about the streets and yards and driveways as if merchants were about to begin a massive winter market: *All items half-price!*

Newt's old injury was acting up, making his limp worse than usual. He stumbled to the corner of a street and sat down heavily, leaned against a fallen pole whose original purpose would forever remain a mystery. In the oddest, most random of occurrences, the words *winter market* had rattled him. He didn't understand fully why. Even though his memory had been wiped long ago, it had always been a strange thing. He and the others recalled countless things about the world that they'd never seen or experienced—airplanes; football; kings and queens; the telly. The Swipe had been more like a tiny machine that burrowed its way through their brains and snipped out the specific memories that made them who they were.

But for some reason, this winter market—this odd thought that had found its way into his musing on the apocalyptic scenes around him—was different. It wasn't a relic of the old world that he knew merely by word association or general knowledge. No. It...

Bloody hell, he thought. It was an actual memory.

He looked around as he tried to process this, saw Cranks of various stages shambling about the streets and parking lots and cluttered yards. He could only assume these people were infected, every one of them, no matter their actions or tendencies—otherwise why would they be out here, out in the open like this? Some had the awareness and normal flow of movement that he still did, early on in that infection, their minds still mostly whole. A family huddled together upon wilting grass, eating scavenged food, the mom holding a shotgun for protection; a woman leaned against a cement wall, her arms folded, crying—her eyes revealed the despair of her circumstances, but not madness, not yet; small clusters of people talked in hushed whispers, observing the chaos around them, probably trying to come up with plans for a life that no longer had plans anyone might desire.

Others in the area were seemingly in-between the first and last stages, acting erratic and angry, uncertain, sad. He watched a man march across an intersection with his young daughter in tow, holding her hand, looking for all the world as if they might be going to a park or to the store for candy. But right in the middle of the street he stopped, dropped the girl's hand, looked at her like a stranger, then wailed and wept like a child himself. Newt saw a woman eating a banana—where had she gotten a buggin' banana?—who stopped midway through, tossed it on the ground, then started stomping it with both feet as if she'd found a rat nibbling at her baby in a knocked-over pram.

And then there were, of course, those who had, without a doubt, traveled well past the Gone, that line in the sand that divided humans from animals, people from beasts. A girl, who couldn't have been older than 15 or 16, lay flat on the ground in the middle of the nearest road, babbling incoherently, chewing on her fingers hard enough that blood dripped back down onto her face. She giggled every time it did so. Not far from her, a man crouched over a chunk of what looked like raw chicken, pale and pink. He didn't eat it, not yet, but his eyes darted left and right and up and down, empty of sanity, ready to attack any fool who dared try to take his meat away. Farther down that same street, a few Cranks were fighting each other like a pack of wolves, biting and clawing and tearing as if they had been dropped in a gladiator's coliseum and only one would be allowed to walk away alive.

Newt lowered his eyes, sank onto the pavement. He slipped the backpack from his shoulders and cradled it in his arms, felt the hard edge of the Launcher he'd stolen from Jorge's weapons stash on the Berg. Newt didn't know how long the energy-dependent, electric-firing projectile device would last, but he figured it couldn't hurt to have it. The knife resided in the pocket of his jeans, folded up, a pretty sturdy one, if it ever came to hand-to-hand battle.

But that was the thing. Like he'd thought earlier, everything he saw around him had become the "new normal" of sorts, and for the life of him he couldn't figure out why he wasn't terrified. He felt no fear, no apprehension, no stress, no innate desire to run, run, run. How many times had he come across Cranks since escaping the Maze? How many times had he almost soiled his pants from sheer terror? Maybe it was the fact that he was now one of them, quickly descending to their level of madness, that stayed his fear. Or maybe it was the madness itself, destroying his most human of instincts.

And what of that whole winter market thing? Was the Flare finally releasing him from the hold of the Swipe he'd been subjected to by WICKED? Could that perhaps be the ticket to his final journey past the Gone? He already felt the most acute and abject despair he'd ever felt in his life, abandoning his friends forever. If memories of his life *before*, of his family, began to invade him without mercy, he didn't know how he could possibly take it.

The rumbling sound of engines finally, mercifully, ripped him from these increasingly depressing thoughts. Three trucks had appeared around the corner of a street that led away from the city, although calling them trucks was like calling a tiger a cat. The things were massive, 40 or 50 feet long and half that in height and width, heavily armored, windows tinted black with steel bars reinforcing them against attacks. The tires alone were taller than Newt himself, and he could only stare, wondering in awe what he might be about to witness firsthand.

A horn sounded from all three vehicles at once, a thunderous noise that made his eardrums rattle in their

10

cages. It was the sound he'd heard earlier from inside the Berg. Some of the surrounding Cranks ran at the sight of the monsters-on-wheels, still smart enough to know that danger had arrived from the horizon. But most of them were oblivious, looking on much as Newt did, as curious as a newborn baby seeing lights and hearing voices for the first time. He had the advantage of distance and plenty of hordes between him and the new arrivals. Feeling safe in the most unsafe of places, Newt watched things unfold—though he did unzip his backpack and place one hand on the cool metal surface of the stolen Launcher.

The trucks came to a stop, the blasting noise of their horns ceasing like a shattered echo. Men and women piled out of the cabins, dressed to the hilt in black and gray, some with red shirts pulled over their torso, chests armored, heads covered with helmets as shiny as dark glass, all of them holding long-shafted weapons that made Newt's Launcher look like a toy gun. At least a dozen of these soldiers began firing indiscriminately, their aim fastened on anyone who moved. Newt didn't know a single thing about the weapons they used, but flashes of light shot from their barrels with a noise that reminded him of Frypan— when he'd bang a heavy stick against a warped piece of metal they'd found somewhere in the nether parts of the Glade. To tell people his latest and greatest meal was ready to be devoured. It made a vibrating *whomp* sound that made his very bones tremble.

They weren't killing the Cranks. Just stunning them, temporarily causing paralysis. Many of them still shouted or wailed after they'd fallen to the ground, and continued to do so as the soldiers dragged them with the least amount of tenderness possible toward the huge doors at the back of the trucks. Someone had opened them while Newt observed the onslaught, and beyond those doors was a cavernous holding cell for the captives. The soldiers must've eaten a lot of meat and drank a lot of milk because they picked up the limp bodies of the Cranks and tossed them inside the darkness as if they were no more than small bales of hay.

"What the hell are you doing?"

A voice, a tight strum of words, came from right behind Newt's ear, and he yelped so loud that he just knew the soldiers would stop everything they were doing and charge after him. He spun around to see a woman crouched next to him, shielded by the fallen pole, a small child in her arms. A boy, maybe three years old.

Newt's heart had jolted at her voice, the first time he'd been startled since coming outside, despite all the horrors developing around him. He couldn't find words to respond.

"You need to run," she said. "They're doing a full sweep of the whole damn place today. You been asleep or what?"

Newt shook his head, wondering why this lady bothered with him if she felt it so important to get out of there. He searched for something to say and found it in the haze that filled his mind lately.

"Where are they taking them? I think I saw a place from the Ber—I mean, I've heard of a place where they keep Cranks. Where Cranks live. Is that it?"

She shouted to be heard over the commotion. "Maybe. Probably. They call it the Crank Palace." The lady had dark hair, dark skin, dark eyes. She looked as rough as Newt felt, but at least those eyes had sanity with a dash of kindness thrown in. The little boy was as scared as any human Newt had ever seen, eyes cinched tight and his arms wrapped around his mum's neck like twisted bars of steel. "Apparently there are people who're immune to the Flare"—Newt bristled at that word, *immune*, bristled hard, but kept silent as she went on—"people who are kind enough or stupid enough or just paid a crap-ton money enough to kinda take care of them at the Palace until they're... you know. Un-take-care-able anymore. Although I heard the place is getting full and they might be giving up on that whole idea. Wouldn't surprise me one damn bit if this roundup ends at the Flare pits."

She said the last two words as if it were something anyone with half a brain knew all about, an image that seemed appropriate for their new world.

"Flare pits?" he asked.

"What do you think the constant smoke on the east side of the city is?" Her response said it all, though Newt hadn't noticed such a thing. "Now, are you coming with us or not?"

"I'm coming with you," he said, each word popping from his mouth without any consideration.

"Good. The rest of my family is dead and I could use the help."

Even through the shock of her words, he recognized the self-serving motive in coming to him; otherwise he would've suspected a trap. He started to ask a question—he didn't know exactly what yet, something about who she was and where they were going—but she'd already turned around and sprinted in a direction away from where the soldiers were still tossing lifeless but living bodies into the hold of the trucks. The wails and cries of anguish were like a field of dying children.

Newt threw his backpack onto his shoulders, cinched the straps, felt the dig of the Launcher against his spine, then took off after this new friend of his and the little one clutched to her chest.

Chapter Three

The woman had more energy than a Runner from the Maze, and those guys ran the corridors, blades, and slot canyons of that beast all day long, day-in and day-out. Newt had gotten out of shape at some point, sucking air until it felt like someone had stolen all the oxygen from Denver with a magical net. His buggin' limp didn't help matters. They'd gone at least a mile before he finally found out her name.

"Keisha," she said as they stopped for a breath inside an old wreck of a neighborhood, right under the skeletal, long-dead branches of a maple tree, almost no other person in sight. Newt felt a little better when she doubled over, chest heaving, to put the toddler down so she could rest. Human, after all. "My kid's name is Dante. You might've noticed he doesn't talk a whole lot—well, that's just the way it is. Not a thing I can do about it, is there? And yes we named him that because of the epic poem."

What epic poem? Newt wanted to ask. He had no idea what she was talking about, though he had a sense of memory knocking on his brain from the other side of a hidden door. Maybe he'd known before the Swipe. He tried not to wonder what might be wrong with her kid that he didn't speak. Traumatized?

Impaired, somehow? Maybe just shy? He wanted to know their stories but wasn't sure he had the right.

"The poem about the nine circles of Hell?" she prodded, mistaking his internal thoughts and musings. "Didn't read too many books in your neck of the woods growing up, huh? Shame. You missed out big time on that one. It's a doozy."

Newt was certain he'd read books, as certain as he knew he'd eaten food and guzzled water before they'd taken his memory. But he didn't remember any of the stories, and the thought filled him with a heavy sadness.

"Why did you name your kid after Hell?" he asked, really just trying to lighten the mood.

Keisha plopped onto her butt and gave little Dante a kiss. Newt had expected the boy to be a brat, cry his lungs out in a place like this. But so far he hadn't made a peep.

"We didn't name him after Hell, you moron," Keisha responded, somehow saying it kindly. "We named him after the guy who *defined* Hell. Who embraced it and made it his own."

Newt nodded, lips pursed, trying to show he'd been impressed without having to lie and say it out loud.

"Corny, I know," Keisha replied after seeing his expression. "We might've been drunk."

Newt knelt next to them, still trying to take in deep breaths without making it too obvious that he needed it so desperately. "Sounds about right. Drunk and corny's the way to go these days." He reached out and gently pinched Dante's cheek, tried to give the kid a smile. To his astonishment, the boy smiled back, showing a mouthful of tiny teeth that gleamed in the afternoon light.

"Ah, he likes you," Keisha said. "Ain't that the cutest thing. Congrats, you're his new papa."

Newt had been squatting, but that comment made him fall backward onto his rear end.

Keisha laughed, a sound as good as birdsong. "Relax, dumbass. You don't look like dad material and it was just a joke. Doesn't matter. We'll all be *Looney Tunes* crazy in a month anyway."

Newt smiled, hoping it didn't look as forced as it felt. Leaves scattered across the pavement of the street as a breeze picked up, making the branches above them go clackety-clack as they banged against each other. He could hear voices and shouts in the distance, seeming to ride on that breeze, but not close enough to panic. They were safe enough for a few minutes, anyway.

He got up his nerve and asked the question that had been on his mind. "You said your family was dead. What did you mean? Did you lose a lot of people?"

"That I did, my fine-haired friend." Keisha had a unique way of saying light-hearted things very sadly. "My hubby. Two sisters. A brother. My old man. Uncles. Aunts. Cousins. And my other... my other..." Here she lost any pretense that the world was still a place where you called people your *fine-haired friend*. Her face collapsed into despair, head literally dropping toward the ground along with it, and tears dropped from her eyes onto the cracked pavement of the sidewalk. Though silent, her shoulders shook with a hitched sob.

"You don't have to say," Newt said. It was as obvious as the sun being hot and the moon being white. She'd lost one of her children. Poor Dante had not been an only child. "I'm... I'm really sorry I asked." *I'm such*

17

a turd, he chided himself. He'd literally known this woman for all of an hour at most.

She sniffed hard, then brought her head back up to look at him, wiping away the tears that had managed to stick to her cheeks. "No, it's okay." She said these words in a distant monotone, somehow wistful and haunted at once. "Just do me a favor. Don't ever ask me—never, ever—how I lost them all. No matter how long we survive or if I know you one day or one month. Never ask. Please." Her eyes, glistening wet, finally met his, the saddest eyes he'd seen since Chuck gave him one last look right outside the Maze.

"Yeah, I promise," he said. "I swear. We don't need to talk about that stuff. I shouldn't have started it."

Keisha shook her head. "No, stop being a worry-wart. Just as long as you don't ask me... you know. We'll be good."

Newt nodded, selfishly wishing he could vanish into thin air and end this awkward, horrible conversation. He gazed down at Dante, who was sitting still and quiet, looking at his mom as if he wondered what was wrong with her. Maybe he wasn't old enough to remember all the bad things that had happened to those who shared his blood.

"What's your plan, anyway?" Keisha asked after a minute or so of silence. "You don't have to tell me your story or anything—fair's fair—but what were you doing lying there like a spent popsicle stick, just waiting for those A-holes to come get you?"

"I..." Newt had absolutely no idea what to say. "I found out recently that I've got the bloody Flare and I couldn't stand the thought of my friends seeing me degenerate into a raving lunatic. Or take the chance that I might hurt them. So I left. Didn't even say goodbye. Well I left a note tellin' them I was gonna go live with the infected—that Crank Palace, I guess, the one you told me about. Oh, and I left another note asking my best friend to kill me if he ever saw me going completely bonkers and—"

He cut off when he realized she was staring at him with giant eyes, no trace of tears left to shine against the fading sunlight.

"Too much?" he asked.

She gave a slow nod. "Too much. I don't even know where to begin. Do I need to be worried, here? You're not gonna try to eat my arm, are you? Or my kid?" She coughed out a fake laugh that made him cringe.

"Sorry. I just... I don't know. I'm not in a good way, I guess."

"Yeah, none of us are. But... what the hell. So many questions. I mean, first off, your friends didn't catch the Flare from you? What, did you escape from inside Denver or something?"

He shook his head. "No, no, it's a long story." He wasn't ready to tell any*one* any*thing* about all the crap he'd been through and that he'd cruelly been thrown in with a bunch of people who were immune to the virus. What would be the point? He and all these people would be dead or past the Gone soon enough.

"Okay," Keisha said slowly, acting now as if she humored the tall tales of a child. She must've had plenty of practice with such a thing. "Then let's fish another fry—"

"Fish another what?"

Her face scowled in rebuke. "You're gonna have to get used to my humor, young man."

He almost protested again—she couldn't be more than 10 years older than him—but he fell silent when her scowl deepened even further.

"Now listen to me and listen to me well. What in *the* hell and what on God's green Earth were you going on about when you said you want to go live with the infected, live at the Crank Palace? I know we're heading toward crazy, now, but we don't seem too ready to get off the train just yet. Or at least I thought so, anyway. But if you're gonna sit here and yap about wanting to go to *that* place, then you were crazy long before you got the Flare. Don't come at me again with something so stupid."

She probably would've kept on going but now it was her turn to stutter to a stop when she saw *his* wide eyes.

"What?" she asked. "You don't believe me?"

Newt stumbled through a few words of nonsense before he got out anything coherent. "Mainly I just wanted to leave my friends behind before I went off the rails. But maybe it's the best place to go. Be with the other sorry saps who're infected. For one thing, maybe they have food and shelter, there, everybody's in the same boat." Newt didn't believe a single word coming out of his own mouth. "What else am I gonna do? Go settle on a farm and raise cattle for the jerks in Denver?"

"Raise cattle for the..." Keisha's words trailed into silence as she shook her head in wonder at the apparent stupidity of his full statement. "Look, I'm just gonna have to treat you like my third child, okay? Deal? I don't have time for this nonsense talk. Now, let's get up and go. The sweeps will probably go all night 'till they can't find another soul to toss into those

20

trucks. They don't like dirty rats like us getting too close to their precious city."

She stood up, helped little Dante stand as well, holding him by the hand. Newt got to his feet, neither in the mood nor having any basis to argue with her anyway. Didn't matter. He was away from Tommy and the others and that had been the main goal all along. Who cared what happened to him now.

Keisha pointed in the direction of the sun, now sinking with earnest toward the horizon, which was hidden by houses and trees and distant mountains in the gaps. "From what I hear we just have to make it a few more miles and we can probably find a house to sleep in. Hopefully some food. Most of the crazies end up congregating like ants around the city so we should be safer the farther out we—"

An electronic charging sound cut her off, a sound way too similar to the charge of a Launcher, which filled Newt with instant dread. He spun around to see three red-shirted soldiers standing there, all of them pointing the barrels of those unwieldy weapons at Newt and his new friend. The blue glow of the guns was bright even in the light of day.

"I need those hands up in the air," one of the soldiers said, the voice coming through a speaker in the helmet. A woman by the sound of it. "You look like decent people, but we need to at least test you and see if—"

"Don't bother," Keisha said. "We've got the damn Flare and you know it. Just let us go. Please? I've got a kid for heaven's sake. We promise we'll just keep walking the other direction—won't bother a soul. We'll never come near the city again. Cross my heart, hope to die, stick a needle in my eye."

"You know we can't do that," the woman replied. "You came too close and you should know better. We want these streets empty."

Keisha made some kind of angry noise that Newt had never heard expelled from a human before, not even a Crank. Something from deep within her chest, like a growl. "Didn't you hear what I just said? We're gonna keep walking *away* from the city. You'll never see us again."

"If that's the case then you won't mind us giving you a lift, will you?" The soldier hefted her weapon to make a point, stepped closer, the barrel now aiming squarely at Keisha's head. "Ya know, this thing will knock you out no matter where it strikes, but shots to the head are especially bad. You'll be puking and seeing double for a week. Now come along nice and easy, got it?"

Keisha nodded. "Oh, I got it."

The next two seconds happened so quickly and yet so slowly that Newt felt as if he'd been transplanted to a dream, where nothing made sense. Keisha had pulled out an old-school revolver from seemingly nowhere, as though it had materialized through a magic spell. Even as her arm jerked up, even as it let out the *pop-pop* of two shots, the soldier who'd been talking ignited her weapon, firing that strange flash of lightning along with its *thwack* of thumped air, an almost silent thunderbolt that was felt more than heard. Blue energy arced across Keisha's face and she screamed a bloody shriek of murder and pain. Her body collapsed to the ground, arms and legs shaking with spasms. Little Dante was less than a foot from her, and for the first time since they'd met, he began to wail like the child that he was. The combined sounds of their anguish—mother and son—were enough to ignite a cauldron of rage inside Newt, coursing through his veins like flooded pipes.

He yelled—a primal, animal yell—and ran for the closest soldier, who stood there as if stunned, doing nothing, his weapon pointed at the pavement. The woman who'd shot Keisha was down on both knees, nursing a wound to her stomach. The third soldier lay flat on the ground, a crimson pool of blood widening beneath his or her bullet-shattered helmet. Newt dove at the only one standing, the one who seemed at a complete loss.

Newt's shoulder crashed into the person's chest, even as the man—at least Newt thought he was a man— shouted a muffled cry for help into whatever communication system the soldiers used. Newt's arms wrapped around him, the momentum of his dive catapulting both of them to the ground in a violent tackle, the other man's weight cushioning the fall. On some level, Newt knew he was being reckless, that an irrational rage had consumed him, that he was being... unstable. But that didn't stop him from screaming again, from sitting back on the soldier's stomach, from reaching forward to grab the man's helmet with both hands and lift it, slam it back into the ground. He lifted it again, slammed it again. This time he heard a crack and a whimpering groan of pain that faded like a last breath.

The soldier's entire body went still.

Newt's breaths were pouring into his chest like a bellows, his chest heaving so much that he almost fainted, almost swooned off the man. But then another kick of adrenaline burst through him. He felt invincible.

Elated. Hysterically euphoric. While still tethered to reality enough to know that the virus was changing him more and more each day. This would be his life soon. Seeking the thrill and feast of enacted rage.

But then something hit him in the back of the head and his brief stint as a warrior ended with him flopping to the ground like a collapsed balloon. He didn't quite fade from the day around him—could just see Keisha lying on the ground with Dante beside her, panicked and bawling—but a few seconds later Newt vomited all over himself.

Why the bloody hell had he ever left that Berg?

Chapter Four

The next hour was a lifetime of headaches, nausea, and strange movements.

Newt stayed awake for all of it; the hyper-enthusiasm he'd experienced for all of two minutes had completely vanished. Spent. He had no energy what-soever, in fact, didn't lift a finger to defend himself as reinforcement soldiers did whatever they wanted with him. At least they didn't separate him from Keisha and Dante. He couldn't bear the thought of losing the small connection he had with those two after so short a time.

A truck rumbled up, much smaller than the behemoths they'd seen earlier by the massive walls of Denver. Two people picked him off the ground, with not the least amount of gentility, and threw him into the back of the open bed of the vehicle. He expected to land on a pile of writhing bodies, a dozen Cranks fighting and clawing and trying to get out. Instead he landed on the hard steel of the truck bed and lost his breath for a moment. Keisha came next, still no sign of voluntary movement in her limbs.

But her eyes.

Her eyes were lit with awareness and understanding, the purest panic Newt could imagine. But that eased a bit when Dante was plopped right next to her, offered a little more care than they'd been given. The kid still cried, but it had almost become a constant, a background noise, like the strong flow of a rapid, rocky river nearby. He laid his head down on his mum's shoulder and wrapped his tiny arms around her neck. Tears leaked from Keisha's eyes.

"She's okay," Newt murmured, though he doubted the kid heard or understood. "She's just... she'll be okay soon." Every word he uttered rang in his head like a broken bell.

A soldier jumped into the back of the truck with them, squatted with his back to the window of the cabin. He held something that looked more like a machine gun than an energy weapon, and Newt figured they had less than one chance left for misbehaving. The next time would be rewarded with a few bullets in the brain to end things.

The truck roared its engine, then set off from the quiet neighborhood—probably quiet because the sweep-up of Cranks had already been through that area. Newt had the distant thought that spying eyes might've reported them from within the windows of one of those seemingly innocent homes, frightened eyes that spied from the darkness, from behind torn curtains and broken glass. Surprised at himself, Newt found that he didn't care. Maybe the virus had eaten that part of his brain first—the part that worried and agonized over what lay in his immediate future. It just didn't matter. Madness awaited him at the end of the track, and there was no slowing that train. He couldn't bring himself to care how bumpy the ride might be.

Newt relaxed onto his back and looked up at the sky as they drove. Blue and white, more clouds than not, the kind with no shape or substance, just scratched across the azure heavens by a painter with no discipline. Some people said the sky never had quite the same color once the catastrophic sun flares struck a couple of decades earlier. Newt would never know, could never know. What he saw seemed natural enough, and despite his sudden indifference to the world, it gave him a small squeeze of comfort that saddened him a little. Saddened that he'd never have a chance to live a full and meaningful life under the skies above.

The truck jostled to a stop sometime later, how long Newt didn't really know. Maybe a half hour. They had parked between two platforms of cement, both seeming to hover just a few feet above the lip of the truck bed, bordered by steel railings. Several people stood up there to each side, dressed in bulky, overbearing protective gear that looked like something you'd see at WICKED on a bad day. Newt quickly glanced at Keisha, who had her back to him, her arms wrapped around her son. She might've been asleep—he saw her back rise and fall with even breaths. He sighed in relief.

Glancing skyward at the strangers staring down, he shifted his elbows to prop himself up. He opened his mouth to say something—ask something—but a fire hose appeared at one of the railings, its nozzle pointing in his direction. It was enough to silence him.

Water—he *hoped* it was water—abruptly flushed out of the hose in a torrid stream, wetly smacking into him so hard that he slammed against the truck bed, yelping at the slicing, biting cold of the onslaught. The force of it was painful enough, but the frigidity made it feel acidic, stinging like a million slaps against his skin.

27

He tried to scream against it, but water filled his mouth and set him off to choking and coughing instead. The person above directed the stream at Keisha and Dante, then, just as he thought he might drown. Keisha seemed completely back to normal because she squirmed and kicked and shielded Dante as best she could. The hose set upon Newt again, then back to Keisha, then back to Newt. This torture lasted another minute or two before some angel turned it off. Newt and Keisha were left to sputter and spit and catch their breath, all amidst the backdrop of Dante's high-pitched screams.

"What the hell was that for?" Keisha yelled, sounding like someone who'd just swam 50 feet underwater and finally came up for air.

A mechanized voice responded, filtered by the hazard suit. "That's the best we can do out here to disinfect. Sorry. We don't have a helluva lot of choices anymore. Hope the kid's okay." With that compassion-dripping statement, he gave a wave of the hand. The truck jolted and the engine squawked, and they were off again.

They picked up speed. With their wet clothes, it felt as if the temperature had dropped 30 degrees. Keisha fully grasped her maternal role and pulled Newt close to her, cradling both him and her son. Dante had gone silent, perhaps shivering too violently to cry. Newt had no complaints, snuggling into Keisha's grasp for as much warmth as possible. He had flashes of a woman in his mind, shadows made of light, no features, more a presence than anything. His mind was loosening, he knew that now, the irony of it so thick it seemed possible to chop at it with an axe. He would remember his mom soon, remember her fully, just in time to forget her in the madness of the Flare.

28

A few minutes later they drove through the opened doors of a gate, providing entrance past a huge wall of wooden planks, a sign on one of the doors that flashed by too quickly for Newt to read the words printed there. Several people stood around, scratches and bruises on their faces, all of them holding Launchers. Not a one looked too thrilled to have visitors. Then there were trees, half of them dead, half of them green and bright and hale. The world was coming back to life, slowly but surely, especially in these higher elevations.

The truck came to a stop again. Barely enough time had passed for Newt's skin to dry, much less his hair or clothes. Both doors of the vehicle opened and closed, and something told Newt their journey was over, that they might never be in another car or truck for the rest of whatever remained of their lives.

"Are you going to kill us?" Keisha asked the empty air above them in a shaky voice, the first time Newt had seen her show genuine fear. "Please don't hurt my children."

Children. Was it her fleeing mind, imagining that Newt was her daughter, come back from the dead? Or did awareness still cling to her strongly enough to hope for more leniency granted a mother and her kids? Before anyone bothered to answer, the three of them sat up, letting go of their temporary cuddle of warmth. Two soldiers stood at the tailgate of the truck, the gate still closed. They were helmeted, their faces nothing but shiny black glass, as soulless as robots. That now-familiar, muffled, slightly mechanized voice came from one of them, a low growl that sounded almost like static.

"You're lucky to be alive," it said. "Especially after

killing my friend. So if you complain I'll beat the living hell out of you. I swear it on all your dead relatives."

"Wow," Keisha said. "Harsh. Wake up on the wrong side of the bed this morning?" Newt was amazed that she had the guts to make even the slightest of jokes.

The soldier who'd spoken gripped the upper edge of the tailgate with gloved fists, the leather creaking as he squeezed. "Say another word. Just one more word. You think this would be the first time we've *accidentally* broken an order? Sure would be a shame for that kid if his mama died because she wasn't... cooperative."

To Newt's immeasurable relief, Keisha didn't respond. She looked at Dante, finding all the strength she needed in his eyes, in his life.

"Just get out of the truck," the other soldier piped in. "Now. You're gonna spend the rest of your life in this hellhole so you might as well make yourselves at home." She pulled on a latch and the tailgate flopped down with a heavy metallic crack.

Newt had a sudden and almost overwhelming rush of panic, the uncertainty of his life now, all at once, taking on meaning again. He moved to deflect it, scooted himself forward until he could jump down from the truck bed onto the ground, a mishmash of dirt and weeds. A quick look around showed a lot of trees and dozens of tiny cabins and tents, as haphazard as the early days of the Glade. Newt felt a longing for his friends and old days past, as hard as those old days were.

Keisha handed Dante to Newt, then jumped down and landed right next to him. It was the first time Newt had held the child, maybe the first time he'd *ever* held someone so young. To his surprise, the kid didn't cry, probably too enticed by his new surroundings, probably still feeling a false sense of elation from the absence of a raging fire hose. Even Newt felt that. It was fresh on his mind, and oddly made everything in the world seem a little brighter because he didn't have a rushing explosion of ice-cold water battering his face.

One of the soldiers closed the tailgate, secured the latch. Then they headed for the doors of the truck without saying anything, opened them, readied to step up and onto the seats.

"Wait," Newt said, handing Dante back to his mum. "What're we supposed to do?"

The soldier on the passenger side ignored them, got in, slammed the door. The driver paused with a foot on the instep, but didn't turn around to face them when she answered.

"Like we said, just be glad you're alive. Hardly anyone's being sent here anymore. Almost full. Most Cranks are just... you know. Taken care of."

The Crank Palace. A sicker version of Newt would've laughed. He'd ended up here after all, even after Keisha's less-than-subtle declaration that it had been the dumbest idea ever.

"But why?" Keisha asked, gently swaying with Dante in her arms. "If you're offing most of the infected, then why not us? After what we did?" There was no apology in her voice. None at all.

"Are you complaining?" the soldier countered. "I'd be happy to take you to the Flare pits if that's what your heart desires. It's what you deserve."

Newt quickly spoke up. "No, no. Thank you. We're fine." He gently grabbed Keisha's arm, tried to pull her away from the truck. He wanted nothing to do with these people ever again. But she resisted, seemed intent on getting them killed or burned in the pits.

"Why?" she asked. "What're you not telling us?"

Even though they couldn't see the soldier's face, every inch of her armored body screamed out what her facial expressions couldn't. Frustration. Annoyance. Anger. But then she relaxed, all of her muscles slackening at once, her foot dropping back to the ground. She turned toward them and spoke with that mechanized voice, void of feeling.

"It's him." She pointed at Newt. "They know who he is and... *she* wants to keep track of him. You and your kid are just lucky you made a new friend. Otherwise you would've been dead long before you made it to the pits. Now goodbye and have a wonderful life. Short and sweet, as they say."

With that, she jumped in the truck and drove off, the back tires spitting up rocks and dirt.

"Who was she talking about?" Keisha asked. "Who is... *she*?"

Newt only shook his head, staring at the truck as it grew smaller with distance. Finally it turned a corner around some trees and was gone. He looked at the ground.

"Later," was the only word that came out.

She.

He couldn't bring himself to say her name.

Chapter Five

Newt didn't grasp their surroundings until after the truck had left, as if his senses didn't fully kick in until they knew they'd been freed from the soldiers and their potential for harm. Without saying much at all, with Dante—asleep now—in her arms, Keisha and he walked around and took stock of the area in which they'd been dumped.

It was a dry, dusty place, although the trees provided enough shade and fallen leaves to dampen the effect. Almost everywhere you looked, signs of habitation filled the spaces and gaps. Small, hastily built cabins, some without windows, some with broken windows. Tents of all sizes that appeared to have been erected weeks or months ago, with old couches or chairs plopped next to their entrance flaps, lines—draped with towels and clothing left to dry—hung from the trees above them, old shoes and bags of trash and small tables scattered hither and thither. Newt once again flashed back to the early days of the Maze, could almost picture the towering stone walls looming somewhere just out of sight.

Several habitations looked less occupied than others, some having been obviously abandoned or never used. Newt took a turn holding Dante—the kid was absolutely zonked after all that adventure and mayhem—and the three of them found a small cabin nestled between two large oak trees. They stood inside of it, taking a tour that lasted about 20 seconds. It was one room, no kitchen, no bathroom, completely empty of possessions or furniture. The lone window, facing east based on the position of the setting sun, had once held glass. Now it held three nasty-looking shards the size of Newt's thumb.

"It's perfect," Keisha pronounced, voice dripping with sarcasm. "And we'll have a nice draft through that busted window. I can't think of anything else I've ever wanted in a home."

Newt realized he was patting Dante's back as if he were a baby. "A couch would be nice. Maybe some food." The whole situation was absurd, and they both knew it. Here they were, acting like a nice little family, settling down in their new home. Maybe a neighbor would drop by soon with a plate of biscuits and a bloody teapot.

"I'm gonna go check things out," Newt said, not even sure what he meant until the words came out. But he couldn't just stand there anymore. No matter how nice it seemed, these people weren't his family and he'd be a fool to throw his lot in with them completely. At least not yet. He needed to explore, see what this Crank Palace was all about.

Keisha gave him a hard glare. "Don't even think about it."

"What?"

"Abandoning us. You're the only friend we've got in this world. And I think you need us as badly as we need you. We *literally* have crazy people for neighbors. You saw all the lived-in places before we found this one. I don't know if they're at a party or what, but they'll be back. Probably carrying torches and pitchforks."

Her words touched him, he had to admit. But he also felt uneasy, fidgety, like something wasn't quite right. He had an inexplicable and sudden urge to yell at her, to tell her to leave him alone, that he could do whatever he wanted. Like a child. Thankfully he resisted.

"I just wanna know what's out there," he said, trying to keep the defensiveness out of his voice. "Sun's almost down, but I'll be quick about it. For one thing, we need something to eat. When's the last time Dante had any food?"

Keisha let out a monstrous sigh of frustration and stepped over to a wall, then turned around, put her back to the cheap wood and slid to the floor. She gently dropped Dante into her lap, where he continued to sleep like he planned to do it straight through the end of days.

"Please wait until morning," Keisha said, as quiet as he'd heard her speak yet. "I can't... Life is hard enough, Newt. I can't bear the thought of being here alone in the dark, terrified out of my wits at what may come walking by, knocking on our door, peeking through our broken window. Breaking through that flimsy door. All that on top of worrying about what the hell you've gotten yourself into out there? Please don't do that to me. I barely know you from a lump of rock, but I can see the goodness in your eyes. We need you. Call me mama, call me mum, call me grandma for all I care. But we need you."

Newt almost shook with confusion. Confusion

35

turning into an anger that made no sense. He closed his eyes and forced himself to breathe. *This bloody virus*, he thought. He'd never know how much was paranoia and how much was the true effect of the thing on his mind. But in that moment he just wanted to scream and pound his chest like a damn gorilla.

"Newt?" Keisha asked, looking up at him from the floor. "You forget how to talk?"

A sudden calm washed over him. A calm he hadn't felt in a long time. The extremes were getting to him, but for the short term he'd take that peace and take it happily. He took the few steps to where Keisha sat and sunk to the floor, trying his hardest to fake a genteel smile.

"You're right," he said. "Walking around the bloody Crank Palace without a map and with the sun about to set sounds like something only a crazy person would do."

A brief moment of silence stretched out, the two of them looking at each other, waiting for the other to react. Then, as if a switch had been flipped, they burst into laughter, a rollicking giddiness that made no sense, which just increased the giggles exponentially. They laughed and they chortled and they even threw in a few snorts. Newt couldn't remember the last time something had struck him as so funny as saying what he'd said. The layers and vicious cycles of irony weren't even worth thinking about.

Crazy person. He was a crazy person, all right. She was a crazy person. And they'd just scratched the surface. The crazy person level would just keep going up and up, and they'd be there to laugh like crazy people as it did.

"Who needs food, anyway?" he said through the hysterics. "You can't feed crazy."

"Right?" Keisha managed to respond. She was laughing so hard that Dante had fallen off her lap and lay sprawled across the floor, snoring like a little bear. This made both her and Newt's laughter reach something that could only be called guffaws. He had tears in his eyes and couldn't remember any of the horrors they'd experienced that day.

God help him, going insane wasn't so bad after all.

Chapter Six

In the middle of the night, someone knocked at their door.

Newt had spent an hour or so writing in his journal before falling asleep in a corner of the small cabin, his back pressed against the joint of the walls. Keisha and Dante had been snoring softly since the sun finally sank beneath the horizon, their manner of deep breathing eerily similar to each other, despite their age gap. It had a soothing feel to it, like an oscillating fan—one of the many tiny memories that keep impeding on Newt's mind.

Sleep had been welcome, those soft snores of his new friends turning into the soft break of ocean waves inside a dream, Newt standing on a beach. Nothing happened in that dream, nothing but the ocean water and blue sky and heat of the sun. But then the knocks came, steady and strong, as unwelcome in the paradise of his dream as if an army of scorpion-like crabs had erupted from the sand and crawled all over his body.

He opened his eyes to the darkness of the cabin, but it took a few seconds more for the dream to fade. The choppy surface of the water became the smooth, cheap plastic of the cabin floor, the blue sky the faintly seen ceiling tiles, the sweet ocean air the stale air of the cabin. The knocks came again and Newt was all at once awake.

He jumped to his feet, stared at the door as if he did it long enough he'd magically see through the wooden slab. Keisha stirred from her position on the opposite wall, rubbing her eyes, still asleep. Newt didn't want her to wake up. He couldn't explain why. Against every instinct that screamed at him from the human depths of his former, rational, reasonable mind, he ran to the door and ripped it open, not bothering with a small crack to see who their intruder might be. Even more irrationally, before he could see who'd come inquiring, he stepped out of the cabin and closed the door behind him. The paramount goal of his life appeared to be letting Keisha and Dante sleep, a notion that made as little sense as his actions.

He'd surprised the knocker at their door, a shadow of a person who'd taken several steps backward at his appearance. When the door clicked shut, a silence like the vacuum of outer space overtook the trees and open areas surrounding them. There was no wind, no insects, no rambunctious owls or other nocturnal creatures, no voices, nothing. Newt said the first thing that popped in his head, whispering with conspiratorial angst.

"It was empty. We can leave if we need to. We don't want any trouble."

More silence. Newt was emerging from the grogginess of sleep, felt refreshed but mortally hungry. His stomach growled, the first sound since he'd spoken. Staring at the dark figure before him, he decided to wait it out, use patience as a weapon. A solid minute passed.

"Is it true?" the stranger whispered, the harsh, gravelly voice of a man who seemed to have chunks of rock stuck in his throat.

Newt didn't know what he'd expected—maybe a raging Crank who stabbed him as Newt heroically fought him off, even as he took his last breath, to save the kid—but someone asking him if it's "true" was not on the list. He decided on a little more patience and didn't respond.

"Well, is it?" The stranger was not one for proper introductions and the exchange of pleasantries.

"Is *what* true?" Newt finally asked, rather needlessly, he thought.

"Are you... ya know. One of *them*?" The bloke desperately needed to clear his throat or get emergency surgery.

A testy annoyance overwhelmed Newt's curiosity. "Can you please just ask me whatever it is you're wanting to ask me?"

"Oh, I'm sorry. Sorry." An apology was yet another thing Newt hadn't expected—the man was full of surprises. "It's just a rumor that's running wild all over the Palace. I had to know. I... have reasons. Are you one of the kids that WICKED has been testing? You wanna talk about rumors—there're all kinds of rumors about *that*, now."

Newt felt a chill. His entire hopes for safety in this place had depended on anonymity, staying quiet, off the beaten path. He also had no idea that the general public knew about the things WICKED had been doing to him and his friends.

The Gladers. The thought made him so overwhelmingly sad in that moment that he almost abandoned his visitor and went back inside.

41

JAMES DASHNER

"It's okay if you don't want to talk about it," the man said into the awkward moment of silence. "It's just that I had a nephew taken by those bastards almost 20 years ago. Never heard from him or about him ever again. I don't know what I was hoping for. I'm sorry."

The man's kindness and gentle ways brought Newt back from the abyss of his feelings. He wished he could see the stranger's face but it was too dark.

"No, it's... it's okay. I'm just a little shocked is all. For one thing, how on Earth do people know that about me? We just got dumped here *today*."

"I think the higher-ups leaked the information so that you'd have some protection. Most people here are in the early stages of the Flare, so they're still smart enough to know not to mess with someone like you."

"What? Why? And what was your nephew's name, by the way?" Even as the words came out of his mouth he knew the answer wouldn't mean anything. They hadn't known each other's real names inside the Maze.

"Alejandro. Did... did you know him?" His voice broke on the last word, coming out as part of a hitched sob.

The name rang a bell for Newt, even though it shouldn't have. He'd heard that name before. Maybe. He now found himself wishing and hoping for just one day with all of his memories—each and every one of those suckers, no matter how heart-wrenching it might be—before he was past the Gone.

"I think I knew him," Newt answered quietly, unsure of what answer would help the most. "I'm sorry... they took my memories. But yes. I'm sure he was there."

The shadow before him collapsed to the ground, first to his knees and then bowing forward on his elbows, as if he were about to pray to Newt like a priest. He let out his sobs, then, crying as hard and loud as a grown man possibly could.

Newt looked around, sure that the sounds would wake Keisha and Dante, not to mention anyone within a half-mile. "Listen, I can tell you what it was like. Maybe that'll help." He couldn't think of anything that would possibly help less. "There's a good chance he's still alive, out there somewhere—some of us escaped. I have friends who're trying to make good things happen."

The stranger looked up sharply at this; Newt saw the briefest hint of reflected light in the man's eyes. But he didn't—or couldn't—speak. He dropped to his elbows again, shaking with his cries.

Newt didn't know if he'd ever had patience in his life, but he certainly didn't have any now, and sadly one thing weighed heavily in his mind.

"Listen," he said. "We can talk about it more. But... do you have any food?"

Chapter Seven

Newt had never been so thankful for the arrival of a complete stranger in the middle of the night inquiring about his long-lost nephew. Food. Glorious food. The man's name had finally been revealed as Terry—the most unlikely name Newt could imagine—and it turned out he did have a reason for his rock-salted voice. As a young man he'd had throat cancer, and surgery to fix it. Before the apocalypse. Newt and Keisha found this out and much more as they had their first neighborhood cookout in the Crank Palace.

Dawn had crept in by the time Newt roused Keisha and her son, explained the situation, and then followed Terry to his shack of a home, which was identical to the hut they'd just left. But it was a little more lived-in. Some worn-out old chairs, a few pictures of people nailed to the walls, the lingering smell of body odor. Luckily they ate outside, in the cool air of morning, with Terry and his wife, Maria. She was quiet and fidgety and said stuff that didn't quite make sense—she liked the word *purple*, of all things. The poor woman was obviously farther along the Flare track than her husband.

"We thought they'd given up on this place a few days ago," Terry said through a bite of grilled beef.

Their neighborhood cookout consisted of a campfire with pieces of meat placed on the ends of sticks and roasted over the flames. Beef and chicken by the looks of it, although Newt never asked. He also didn't care. It tasted delicious—he was on his third piece and had no plans to stop anytime soon.

"What do you mean?" Keisha asked as she broke off a chunk of blackened cow innards and fed it to Dante.

Terry shrugged. "You know. This whole getup was originally meant to be a civic service, back in the days when the higher-ups had time to worry about anything but saving their own hides. But once we got full, they stopped dropping people off. Word is they're just burning them in massive pits on the east side of the city. Maria says it's over there because the wind tends to come from the west. They don't wanna smell burning bodies all day long in the city."

"They're purple," Maria said in response, her mouth full. "They're all purple. Purple when they go in, purple when they come out."

Keisha's eyes widened. "Damn, woman. What's your—" She stopped before saying something she'd regret, as if she'd temporarily forgotten that this was what happened—people lost their minds. "Sorry," she muttered under her breath.

"Purple." Maria said it wistfully, staring into the fire. She was a strong woman with calloused hands and leathery skin, her hair turning fast to gray. Terry actually looked just about the same, his hair just a little shorter with a balding patch on the upper deck. If he hadn't introduced her as his wife, Newt might've thought them siblings.

"But then you came along," Terry continued, ignoring Keisha's comment. "We saw the truck, saw you get out, saw them acting like jerks. Saw them drive off. That's when we ran into town to tell people but somehow they already knew. Knew who you were, too. Strange times, getting stranger."

Newt thought about that, chewing his food like such a thing might never happen again. "I don't know why they'd give a crap about me. I'm not immune like most of them. They just had me along for the ride, nothing but a bloody control subject. Once I caught the Flare, my days of being important were long gone. Who knows. They probably just need to know how I end up so they can finish off some stupid report that no one'll ever read." He wondered about this town Terry mentioned, and what such a place would be like.

Keisha spoke up. "You guys seem pretty early in the game, like us. What about all the people further along, especially past the Gone? Where are they?" She shot a quick and sheepish glance at Maria.

"Things can get... pretty brutal," Terry replied. He looked at a piece of charred beef that he'd just been ready to plop in his mouth, lowered it with an expression of disgust. Newt didn't really want to know what knowledge or memory had brought on that transition. "Some are around, and you gotta be careful. Some get taken care of. Some take care of themselves. And once a week or so there's a group—of people like us, not the higher-ups—who round up some of the worst ones and sneak them out of the Palace. I don't know where they take them or what they do with them. Don't want to."

He tossed the uneaten beef back onto his plate. For a few seconds he fought back tears.

"We live in Hell," Keisha said quietly, barely heard over the crackling of the flames.

Newt was tired. Terry had come a-knockin' at their door at least a couple of hours before dawn, and it wasn't as if Newt had slept like a fat and fed baby until that point, what with the bare wooden floor and unfamiliar surroundings. He closed his eyes, wanted nothing more than to crawl closer to that fire, curl up, and sleep the day away. Mainly, the world of dreams seemed a better prospect at the moment than hearing more from Terry. The look he'd given that meat... The lost tone in his voice when he said a group of them rounded up Cranks past the Gone and took them someplace. It was all so ominous. So depressing. His future.

"You look like you could use a nap," Keisha said.

Newt just nodded, mumbled something unintelligible on purpose.

Maria screamed.

Newt jolted awake, looked up at her. She'd jumped to her feet, eyes wide with terror, letting out hysterical shrieks as if someone had poured a family of spiders down the back of her shirt, waving her arms about like a gorilla on the rampage.

"Maria!" Terry yelled. He crawled over to her, grabbed one of her flailing hands, tried to pull her back down to the ground. But she brushed him off, smacked him in the forehead.

"She was *purple*, don't you get it!" She stilled herself, stood rigid with fists at her side like a child demanding something from her parents, took each of them in with a glare. "I didn't even have a chance to raise her! How could I? In this mucked-up world? How could I dare? Better purple than crazy! Better purple than eaten by some damned Crank! Better purple than taken by WICKED and thrown in a cage! Like an animal!"

The words had spilled out of her, one on top of the other, until they blended into a long slur of madness. She sucked in a breath, now, then belted out one last roar, her face reddening and swelling up like a cooked grape.

"*PUUUUUUURPLE!*"

Maria *dove* into the fire. Screaming now from pain more than rage, she slapped at the burning logs, the glowing-hot coals, the ashes turned to gray but still smoldering with intense heat. Newt could *see* the burns melting her skin, right before him, too frozen in shock to help. Her face grew taut, the pain evident, the indifference plainer.

Terry tackled her with such force that both of them tumbled and rolled out of the fire and several feet away. Newt had to lurch to his left to avoid getting smacked by their bodies. When he looked over his shoulder Terry swatted with open palms at any lingering flames that had sprung up on her clothes. Her hair, too. Singed and sooty. It smelled terrible.

Keisha held tightly to Dante, smothering his face into her chest, her own eyes squeezed shut as if not seeing would make it all go away. Terry had stopped pounding on his wife, now just cradled her body and stared down at her, breathing heavily; tears streamed down his face, but he said nothing. Maria lay still, silent, somehow sobbing without noise.

Newt's stomach had turned sour, his weariness gone. He didn't know how badly she'd been burned, but something told him there wasn't a Crank Palace

Hospital up the street, right next to the grocery store and bowling alley.

Terry finally slouched to the side of Maria, crossed his legs pretzel-style, shoulders slumped, forearms on his knees, hands dangling like ornaments. He gave Newt a look that said it all.

Don't ask.

Not that he needed to. The window onto Maria's life had cleared a bit, some of the grime washed away. The only thing left to wonder was which had come harder. The madness it took to kill your own child or the madness that resulted from killing your own child. And at what stage did the Flare creep its way into the affair? Newt had no right to know, and swore to himself he'd never ask.

Newt got to his feet and walked around the fire to where Keisha and Dante huddled together.

"You okay?" he asked lamely.

Keisha nodded but didn't say anything. Dante was quiet as a church mouse, a phrase that popped into Newt's head unbidden, a thing he'd heard a hundred times in the past from someone he loved but couldn't remember. But it was coming back. An image was starting to form. An image of a woman who looked a lot like him.

"I have to go," he said.

This got Keisha's attention. She looked up at him. "What? Go where?"

"I won't be long," was all he gave her in return.

He expected her to argue, but she seemed to understand. "We'll be okay."

Newt had already turned around, was already walking away.

Chapter Eight

He walked 10 minutes before he saw another soul, and the stroll calmed down his nerves. Seeing a lady with so much grief that she jumped into a hell-hot fire, swatted at burning logs and coals like flies on a picnic table... Well, that was enough to make a person wanna take a walk. The morning air had warmed a bit, the sun shining through the leaves of the trees to dapple the ground with dancing light. He took three deep breaths, in through the nose, out through the mouth. He felt better.

And it hadn't taken long to get the lay of the land.

The entire Crank Palace had been designed in a pattern of circles. Sections of rings, bordered on both sides with circular roads or dirt paths. They grew smaller as he walked, gradually; he imagined an astronaut of old might compare it to seeing the Earth's horizon take on its curvature as you rose higher toward space in your rocket ship. And from way up there, Newt figured the Palace must look like a giant game of darts, a bull's-eye in the middle. That bull's-eye was where he headed, and he heard a general clamor of noise coming from that direction.

Another memory leaked out of his Swiped mind—watching a football game on the telly, hearing the roar of the crowd when a striker kicked a goal. It couldn't have been a thing happening in real time; it was a match recorded long ago by his... mum. Yes, his mum. He remembered watching it, clearly.

And the sound of that crowd was what he heard now, increasing in volume with every step. The central hub of the Palace must be a gathering spot of sorts; a large group of people definitely awaited him there, as if he were a gladiator about to step into the Coliseum of ancient times. His wiser half told him to turn around, to at least convince Terry or Keisha to go along with him. But that wasn't going to happen. Newt needed to know what he'd gotten himself into.

Each diminishing ring of land that he passed grew more crowded with tiny cabins, shabby huts, and tents—although there were far fewer of those, now—squeezed in amongst trees, the ground littered with trash. He had a sense that his captors had purposefully dropped them off in a spot still considered the outskirts of the Crank Palace, not fully developed yet—probably planned at one point but abandoned. Most of the structures had broken windows, the glass long missing by the looks of it. He could only assume that shards of glass were the chief weapon around these parts.

He didn't see many people—just a few spotted here and there, mostly a quick glimpse of their backs as they disappeared into whatever shack they considered their home, closing the door behind them. He heard a lock engage every now and then, wondering what good they did in such shabbily built structures. More than a few sets of eyeballs peered out at him as he walked by, giving him the shivers. He chided himself for not grabbing his Launcher before taking the walk; he could've kept it hidden inside the backpack. Right then he'd settle for the knife he also left behind and considered searching the area for a stray piece of glass.

Before his next thought could collect itself, a man stood in front of him, seemingly appearing out of nowhere. He had a glazed look in his eyes, staring at Newt but more like he stared *through* Newt, into some other-worldly distance that made him happy. He had a look of...

Bliss.

Bliss.

Newt's own mind did something like hiccup inside his skull. The memories that continued to strain against the dam of the Swipe bulged outward, for a moment mixing with his recent recollections. He knew what the Bliss was. A drug given to the Flare-infected that was supposed to stall the effects and symptoms of the brain-destroying disease. Looking at this man in front of him, swaying on his feet as if to some unheard tune, eyes glossed over, an expression of delirious glee on his face, Newt wondered. Maybe the drug just got you high so you could forget for a while. Who knew? Newt had stopped walking but started again, stepping around the stranger.

"Don't you want some?" the man asked. "I heard they're gonna stop giving it out soon. Better get it while you can."

Without any shame, with complete awareness that he was the kind of person for whom the drug had been intended, Newt said, "Yeah, I want some. Got any?"

The man made a weird noise that might've been a chuckle. "Now why in the hell would I have asked you that if I didn't have any?" Another chuckle, snort, whatever that sound was that came out of his nose with a little spray of snot. "How much you got to pay for it?"

"How much I got?" Newt sighed. "I got nothin'."

53

The man took an exaggerated step toward the side of the path, squared himself on his feet, then swept forward in a ridiculous, grand bow, one hand crossed over his belly, the other rising up behind him.

He spoke to the ground. "Then I'm sorry to have disturbed you, my good man. As you were."

"As I was," Newt muttered.

He walked toward the crowd noise that hovered in the air like smog.

* * *

No one else bothered him, at least not directly. He certainly *saw* some things that bothered him.

A naked woman clung upside down to the lowest branch of a tree, her arms and legs wrapped around the bark-scratchy wood above her. She made no noise, made no noticeable effort to let herself down, but followed Newt with her eyes as he hurried to scoot past her. There were enough bare-knuckled fights breaking out on the streets and between the huts to keep him entertained if he got bored. A man sat on one of the rings of streets, filthy beyond measure, his back rigid and straight as he sang a soft tune of gibberish. Nearby, two women stood facing each other, staring into one another's eyes, saying nothing, completely still. At their feet lay a man looking blissfully at the sky. Literally with the Bliss, judging by the false glee in his eyes.

These sights increased the farther he went, discouraging him with each step, until he finally came upon a wall, maybe 12 feet high. Unlike the barrier that bordered the Crank Palace as a whole, this wall wasn't made up of wooden planks, nailed together.

This one was cement, or stucco, once painted but now a patchwork of crusty flakes of pastels. An archway stretched over an opening in the wall, which led to the crowd he'd been hearing on the other side, a swath of people milling about like giant, fired-up ants. At the top of the opening's arch, there was a sign with bright letters that seemed as out of place as a kindergarten— from which it very likely might've been stolen— would have been in that nasty place.

CENTRAL ZONE

Newt paused, looking at the sign. Maybe he should go back. Hadn't he learned enough for one day? Wouldn't he feel safer with a weapon or a friend? Yes and yes. But he walked through the archway regardless, into a sea of frantic activity.

The "zone" was wide and circular, just as he'd imagined—the bull's-eye of the Crank Palace from above. Along its outer edge, a ring of dilapidated shops, offices, and restaurants faced inward, most of them looking like they hadn't run a respectable business in years. Where once windows and doors had resided, there were now only empty spots of darkness or hastily nailed-up boards. The glass had been taken long ago. Not many eligible signs remained, either, though one said, in clear black letters against a white background, "Howard's Hoagies: The Best Sammies in the Valley!"

Hundreds of people jammed the paved central area, every last one of them either busy with activity or busy making a beeline for some undisclosed location for some undisclosed purpose. There was lots of yelling, lots of laughing, lots of talking, lots of arguing. In no surprise whatsoever, Newt saw at least seven brawls from where he stood at the entrance. These were often broken up by plain-clothed people holding full-sized Launchers, people who appeared healthier and stronger than those around them. Calmer, a more rational bearing. Or maybe it was just because they were the ones holding weapons—Newt assumed these were the Munies, those immune from the Flare, that worked here either for money or out of the goodness of their precious little hearts. Keisha had mentioned them in their very first conversation but he'd never followed up on it because they'd spent the next hour running for their lives from the Crank sweeps.

It was weird that there were other people like Tommy, Minho, Teresa, and the rest, who for some reason stayed stable and sane despite the viral intrusion. Immune. It shouldn't be weird—of course there were others out there, statistically speaking. Maybe it just rubbed him the wrong way because he was still distraught that he hadn't been the same as his friends. He had a sudden itch to write in his journal, to share some of these feelings. Tonight. Pausing to take another deep breath, he marveled at how much and how quickly he was changing. He felt like an old, sentimental geezer in moments like this.

Movement, a blur that approached in his peripheral vision from the right, snapped him out of it. A woman ran up to him, a middle-aged, short-haired lady with a wrinkly face and bright-blue eyes. She swatted him on the upper arm and kept running, didn't say a word to him. Such things didn't seem to faze anyone else in the huge clearing.

Welcome to Crank Palace, he thought. *Welcome to the Central Zone.*

Welcome to your future.

Chapter Nine

Ignoring his suddenly intense desire to run, to go back to Keisha and Dante, to huddle up in a tiny cabin far away from this madhouse, Newt forced himself to walk the perimeter. Tried to hide his limp as much as possible. He liked to think he was brave, but he felt the fear of so much unpredictability, swirling all around him like the waters of a raging ocean, sharp rocks hidden beneath the dark, white-capped surface.

The former businesses he walked past had a variety of functions, a few only needing a quick glance to know he should just move right along. Drug dens and the like. A lot of the others had become informal eateries, usually a couple of those Launcher-bearing guards keeping watch on the inside to make sure things didn't get out of hand—it was an unstable trifecta, indeed: Cranks, food, hunger.

Newt stepped into the next foodie place he came across because it was mostly empty on the inside. A man stood behind a grill—like something you'd find at a *real* neighborhood cookout, Newt supposed—seemingly not caring that only about half the smoke from the meat he cooked escaped through the open windows in the front. The rest hovered like a mini-weather system along the ceiling of the establishment. Newt coughed a couple of times, then asked a guard standing nearby how much it cost to eat there.

The man was either chewing on some of the goods himself or smacking on gum. He had a Launcher strung over his shoulder and looked as bored out of his mind as one can be.

"Huh?" he asked, trying to make that single word sound as rude as possible.

"I just got here," Newt responded, smart enough to avoid any kind of arrogant display. "How does... money work around here? How can I earn some to buy food?"

The man swallowed—Newt could actually *hear* the gulp of it. "Officially? There ain't no money. This place is welfare, man, didn't you get the post in your hotel room?" He laughed at that but stopped when Newt didn't join in. "Old Leroy here will give you a bite or two. He's one of the best around, cooks like his grandmammy taught him, no doubt. But sniff around the Palace a bit and you'll, uh, how do I wanna say it, you know... *Improve your circumstances*. Yeah, there ya go. There ain't no money but you can definitely be poor. Know what I mean, big guy?"

Newt just shook his head and said, "No."

"Well, ain't you a lot of fun. Get some food before I decide to kick your ratty blond-haired ass out of here. Get on, now. I ain't in the mood to talk to no Cranks, anyhow."

Newt understood survival. He understood it more than most.

He happily accepted a plate of food and chowed it down, even though he'd eaten just an hour or two earlier. It was beef again. Chicken again. Apparently the Crank Palace had no idea what a fruit or vegetable was. As Newt took his last couple of bites and wiped his mouth with a scrawny, half-wet napkin, he had an amusing but very apt question pop into his mind.

Where in the hell were they getting all these cows and chickens?

* * *

Something had switched in his mind and he was ready to leave. He hated the sinking feeling of uncertainty that consumed him—could he go back to that shack and live unhappily ever after with Keisha, Dante, Terry, and a crazy woman with burns all over her hands and knees? Really. What was he going to do here? What was the plan? He'd staved it off for a while, but those hated fingers of despair were clutching at his heart. But in the immediate future of the next 30 minutes, an hour, the rest of the day... He just wanted to be with familiar people again, no matter how slight the *familiar* part of the equation might be.

Walking quickly, now, he hurried to finish his circular sojourn around the Central Zone.

A few more eateries. A gym for boxers—an idea that shone supreme if they could just get the brawlers off the paved clearing and into the makeshift ring they'd set up inside. A market with crafts and odds and ends. A library—a place so crammed with books and ratty but cushioned chairs that it seemed the very definition of cozy; Newt swore to come back there soon. Keisha would love it; he had no doubt. Another location was packed wall to wall with bodies; at first Newt recoiled, thinking it a morgue or mortuary, but he soon saw the bodies... *moving*. They were clothed in odd apparel, writhing on the floor to bizarre music. Dance club? A cult? He hightailed it out of there.

And then there was the bowling alley. He couldn't believe it. Earlier he'd made a joke in his mind about such a thing being in the Crank Palace, but there it was—although there hadn't been a whole lot of bowling going on for a very long time. A joke, after all. Newt had no memory whatsoever of holding a bowling ball, much less playing the game. And yet he understood what it was in concept, had images in his mind of the activity in full swing. But here, the wooden lanes used for such play had been torn up, stacks of them scattered toward the far sides, where people manned actual fires in the niches where bowling pins once stood. They'd probably burned those, too. Sleeping bags, blankets, people lay everywhere. Maybe it was that long line of makeshift fireplaces, but the gloomy place had a cozy warmth similar to the library that made him want to come back. And no one was fighting, at least at the moment.

Newt left through the open door—based on the rusted, dangling hinges, the actual door had been tossed in some distant past—and headed toward the big arch, the exit. Along the way, he was jostled, bumped, hugged, pushed, fell down twice, was helped up once. He caught sight of immunes glaring at him, their Launchers held rigid in their arms, whispering to other Munies, sharing secrets. He couldn't understand what value WICKED saw in making sure that people knew who he was, what he'd been through, and that he'd arrived at the hottest club in town for Cranks. He had to get out of that place. He needed sleep.

Finally he made it to the arch, went under the

bright-colored letters of its sign, half-running and fully relieved to be on the relative quiet of the path that lead to the outer rings of the Palace. He slowed himself to a brisk walk, realized he was completely covered in sweat and that his face felt like it'd been roasted by the sun for hours. Yes, he definitely needed sleep. Maybe a solid 24 hours of it.

He stopped.

Three raggedy-looking Cranks stood in his way, each one holding a steel pipe, as if they'd just robbed the same plumbing store for makeshift weapons. Newt thought he must really be losing his mind because the sight of them made him laugh. It was stupid. Comical. Like something from a 10-year-old's vision of the baddest people on Earth. One of the Cranks even had a bandana tied around his head and affected an evil grin that made him look like he had something wrong with his lips.

"I'm not in the mood," Newt said. He knew with absolute certainty that he could pass a lie detector test right there on the spot, declaring to the officiator that he'd be perfectly okay with these idiots putting him out of his misery.

But fate decided not to call his bluff, at least not yet.

One of the thugs—a man with long, greasy black hair and muscles bulging out of the rips in his shirt—walked up to Newt and stopped about three feet in front of him. Every instinct and internal alarm told Newt to run like hell, but he couldn't bring himself to do it. The ever-expanding crazy part of his brain urged him to lash out and punch the guy in the nose, get the brawl started and hope for the best. Instead, he waited.

"We know who you are," the man said, finally. For such a tough-looking fellow, he sure had a soft voice. The word *velvety* came to Newt's mind and he had an absurd urge to laugh.

"Out with it, then," Newt muttered. "Who am I?"

Surprisingly, the man took on a somewhat humbled air. "We know the things they did to you. To the ones taken. We know the utter shite you've been through. At no choice of your own, trying to find a cure for the likes of us. We're here to tell you that it's... appreciated. That people like us honor you."

Newt swallowed, rendered speechless. This man didn't appear to have any intent of beating the tar out of him, after all. That, or this was all a ruse to... what? Catch him off guard? Nonsense. These blokes could take him down without breaking a sweat.

"Sorry," the man said. "A tad on the cheesy side. We're just..." He straightened his back, lifted his chin a little. "Hell, man. We just wanted you to know that a lot of us are on your side. No one will mess with you. Not until they get through us, first, anyway. I don't know what else to say. I kinda feel like an ass."

Newt nodded, a little thrown off balance but honestly thrilled at the prospect that he might have his own personal security detail.

"Thank you," he replied, worried anything more elaborate might shatter the whole deal.

The man nodded back, then looked around awkwardly as if he hadn't thought this far ahead when he'd imagined the scenario. He stepped to the side of the path, gestured for his two partners to do the same. They did.

"My name is Jonesy," he said. "Well, that's what

they call me anyway. Just give a holler if you need us for anything. We'll always be right around the bend."

"Okay," Newt replied, knowing he could never fully trust a few Cranks holding pipes. But he didn't want them as enemies, either. That was for sure. "Thanks, again. Seriously. Thanks."

Neither the man nor his friends responded, so Newt set off for the outskirts of the Palace again, feeling their eyes on his back as he walked. *We'll always be right around the bend*, the stranger known as Jonesy had said.

Maybe that was the best news yet for Newt since arriving at the Crank Palace.

Or maybe it was the worst. One of those two, for certain.

He walked a little faster.

Chapter Ten

No one else bothered him or talked to him as he made his way back to the pathetic little cabin in which they'd slept the night before. He barely saw anyone at all, even in the peripherals. When he swung by the shack of Terry and Maria, they were sitting in ragged chairs just outside the front door. Maria had been bandaged on her arms and legs with something that looked like a bedsheet torn into strips. Terry gave Newt a half-hearted wave but then stared at the ground; Maria had her eyes closed. The message was clear: you're not invited.

When Newt finally reached his own little hut, he saw Dante—composed, quiet, playing with a rock—sitting by himself on the grass-patchy dirt, the door closed behind him. A terrifying thrill of panic leaped in Newt's nerves, knowing for certain that Keisha would never leave the kid alone like this. Newt sprinted for the door, ripped it open, saw with a sinking heart that it was empty. Even his backpack was gone. His journal. His Launcher. Keisha's things. All of it. Gone.

He lost his balance, felt like he might faint. Leaning against the edge of the doorframe, he forced himself to breathe. Where in the hell had she gone?

No, idiot, he told himself. *Someone took her, took your things.* He sucked in a lungful of air, then turned to Dante. Although he'd never heard the boy speak, he asked him the question anyway.

"Dante, do you know where your mum is? Your mom? Where'd she go?"

No answer, but the kid looked up at him with the saddest look of hope in his eyes. Probably just hearing the word *mom* had stirred something on the inside. Newt tried to shake some reason into his head, felt like the world was literally splitting apart around him, an earthquake, the big one, shaking the whole planet just to make things perfectly apocalyptic.

He made a quick run around the hut to see if she lingered somewhere close. Maybe she'd found a better home for them. Or was looking for one.

No, idiot, he chided himself again. He'd never once seen her—even though it had been only a day or so—never seen her let the boy out of her sight. He walked back to Dante, picked him up, hefted him in his arms until it felt comfortable.

"Don't worry, mate," he said. "We're gonna find your mom."

He allowed himself five seconds to consider in which direction he should go. Toward the Central Zone? Toward the gate that exited the Crank Palace? The latter, he thought. If for no other reason than it was closer and it'd be a good place to start canvassing his way back through the rings of huts and hovels and tents.

"Come on, kid. Let's go."

* * *

The anxiety cinching up his insides with each and every step proved to be almost unbearable. The maddening uncertainty of it was enough to make his heart strain for every single beat. He had to know where she was, what had happened, an outcome, any outcome. He almost dropped Dante with the anguish that consumed him. What in the bloody hell was he going to do if he didn't find her?

But then, there she was.

It was a sight that did a strange thing. In the same moment, he felt an overwhelming relief even while his hopes for the future sunk to the depths of the Earth.

Keisha was fine, at least physically. Keisha was alone.

She walked along, her back to him, slowly and with a lurch in each step, about 200 yards or so from the gate in the huge wooden wall. She had Newt's backpack strapped to her shoulders, her own pack slung in the crook of her left elbow, and with her right hand she dragged along a canvas bag full of what, he didn't know. It had been easy to catch up with her because she moved at a snail's pace, taking a strange little pause to pull on the canvas bag between every two steps, as if the stuff in there weighed more than she did.

"Keisha!" he yelled. She either didn't hear him or pretended not to. He quickened his gait to a run. "Keisha! Stop!" She didn't.

Newt caught up with her, went past her, until he was directly in her path and stood there, facing back, feet planted, holding Dante in front of him like an omen to shame her for the outrageous decision she'd made to leave. She saw them and stopped, although the expression on her face didn't change—she looked exhausted and weary, void of emotion, sweat soaking her hair and skin.

"Keisha," Newt said, trying to dampen the sudden anger he felt. "What on Earth?"

She dropped the end of the canvas sack she'd been dragging. Then she let the pack hitched in her elbow slide down her forearm and into the dirt with a puff of dust. Finally, with an air of defeat, she slipped Newt's backpack off each shoulder and let it slump to the ground. Newt heard the clank of his Launcher, and had the intense hope that his journal was safely inside. She stood there, hunched over a bit, catching her breath.

"I knew he'd be safe with you," she whispered.

The look that then came to her face melted away Newt's anger. A purity of sadness. Her eyes, her mouth, her ears, her cheeks, they all dropped toward the ground, as if they'd just remembered the law of gravity.

"What's going on?" Newt asked. "Where are you going? How could you leave Dante?"

The boy was squirming and Newt finally let him down. He ran to his mom, who overcame her madness long enough to drop to her knees and embrace her only living child in this world. She hugged him fiercely and he hugged her back. Tears poured from her eyes.

"I'm so sorry," she whispered. "I'm so sorry." She said it over and over.

Newt didn't know what else to do but sit on the ground, himself. How was he supposed to approach this incomprehensible situation? What was he supposed to say? Nothing came to mind so he stayed silent, watched the reunion that never should've happened. She'd left her kid. Could her mind really have slipped so much, so quickly?

A minute or two passed. Nothing changed. Keisha finally broke the silence, with a sentence so unexpected and void of context that she had to say it twice.

"I have a cell phone."

"Huh?"

"I have a cell phone."

Chapter Eleven

Newt had never had a cell phone. Like many things in his weird, swiped mind, he knew what it was, of course, that it had been extremely common in the world before the apocalypse. But it had become almost a thing of the past, something forcefully replaced by physical landline or radio communications in a broken world.

Keisha seemed to think her answer sufficient to explain why she'd left her kid behind, stolen Newt's things, and headed for the exit.

"Okay," Newt said, leaning forward on his elbows, their bony tips pressed into his folded legs beneath him. "You have a cell phone. So... what? Does that mean you work for WICKED? You're some kind of evil agent for some evil doctor that's come to study me? One of the infamous Gladers? Is that it?"

The questions were enough to snap Keisha back to reality a little. "Huh? What in the world are you talking about?"

"Why do you have a cell phone?" Newt asked with swelling impatience.

Keisha shrugged. "My husband stole it. A month or so before he... Nevermind. I swore I'd never tell you that story, didn't I?"

"Not really. You just made me promise never to ask about it. I haven't."

"Right." She looked at him for a long time. Dante did as well, something like a smirk on his face, which made Newt feel the slightest bit better. "Anyway, the point is that I have a cell phone."

Newt threw his hands up in frustration. "*Why* is that the point, Keisha?"

"Because it works. I only turn it on once a day to save the battery, then turn it right back off again. Times have been few and far between when I've been able to charge the damn thing."

Newt had something build in his chest, a physical lump of awareness, making it hard to get a full breath. "Someone called you? Sent you a message?"

Keisha nodded with overt exaggeration. "Yes, someone did, Newt. Someone most certainly did."

When she didn't add anything to that, he threw his hands up again. "*Who?*"

Keisha sighed, bent down to kiss Dante on the head. When she looked back up at Newt, it seemed to him like she was trying to make an important decision in her mind. He tried to remember that the mind in which she was working so hard might not be firing on all cylinders, something his dad used to—

Something his dad used to say. Images began flashing through Newt's mind, blurry glimpses of people. His dad, his mum, his... sister. He squeezed his eyes shut and shook his head violently. He couldn't do this right now. He didn't even know if they were sane thoughts. He didn't want to go mad, yet.

"You okay?" Keisha asked. It could almost be funny—now *she* was worried about *him*. Crazy worrying about crazy.

"Yeah," he said quietly. "Yeah."

"You need to take care of Dante for me."

Newt glared. "Take care of him? I'd ask if you'd gone insane but I already know the answer."

"I knew you wouldn't agree to it if I just asked like this. That's why I fed him and left him, knowing you'd be back soon. If not you, then Terry and Maria. I also scrounged up a lot of food and left a bag of it buried right behind the cabin. You probably didn't see my note to you. That's plain as day."

"Nope," Newt replied, his voice listless. "Not nary a note to be seen." He nodded at the canvas bag she'd been dragging. "Is that food, too?"

Keisha nodded.

"Can you please just tell me what's going on? I can't see any explanation of you leaving him behind that could possibly make sense. Not to mention why you'd steal my stuff."

Keisha stared at him, chewing on that for a few seconds. "Fair enough. Let's go over to those trees so that we don't have nosy Munies with Launchers come by asking questions dumber than yours."

Newt agreed, helping her carry all the stuff to a shady spot mostly hidden from the path.

"If you think my questions are dumb," he said, throwing all the snark he could into the words, "then that proves you've lost it. You left your own *kid*, Keisha. I think I have a right to ask you any stupid question I want."

"I know, I was just kidding. Really. I can't help being a smart-ass, even when the world's gone to pot. I'm sorry."

Newt set their things against a thick tree then plopped to the ground, leaning against the clunky backpacks. Keisha sat nearby, Dante in her lap. The day was warm and bright, offset by a breeze that cooled any sweat popping through Newt's skin.

"I left you some clothes and your journal," Keisha said. "It's all in the bag that I buried."

Newt shook his head. "That's great, but it doesn't quite make up for leaving Dante behind. It makes it worse, actually! Shows that you were thinking straight enough to worry about me. But not Dante? I mean... I don't even know what to say."

"Fine, I get it Newt. I'm horrible. Can I tell you my story, now?"

"Yes, Keisha. Please tell me your story. I'm all ears."

She eyed him at that but let it go—she hardly had room to complain at his sarcasm.

"Listen. I came up here with Dante earlier today. They told me I couldn't leave, obviously. I begged and begged. They said no, and quite honestly seemed to have a good time doing it. They kept making the point that if their bosses found out a child was freed from here, every last one of 'em would be fired and probably thrown in jail. Kids are the future and all that crap. Pure BS. I was pretty distraught by this point, Newt. Pretty desperate. I asked if they'd let me go if I left the kid behind and promised to come back. Collateral, I guess."

"Collateral."

She nodded. "But they said I'd have to... earn it. Do them a favor or pay them money, something. That's why I went around like a damned burglar and stole as much food as I could find from every hole of a home I had time to sneak into. And brought as many of our belongings I thought we could do without. I left

74

you your knife and your journal, some clothes, but hopefully I can buy my way out with the rest of this crap, the food, the Launcher, whatever." She gestured at the backpacks and canvas bag that lay piled behind Newt's back.

He didn't like the implications behind some of Keisha's words but also knew it wasn't his place to interfere. But leaving Dante with him without even asking... He decided to leave that for now.

"Okay, I get all that," he said. "But *why*, Keisha. What's going on? Where exactly are you trying to go?"

"It's a sad story, Newt. It's the saddest story I can imagine. I sure wouldn't be able to make up such a thing. You sure you wanna hear it?"

A few seconds earlier, Newt had been insisting on it. Now he wasn't so certain. But he had no choice. "Maybe just give me the short version."

She snorted a laugh. "The short version, huh? Okay, that's a deal. Here it is—my bastard of a husband killed almost every person I've ever loved in my entire sorry life. How's that for short and sweet?"

Newt couldn't look her in the eyes. Why didn't she just leave Dante with someone else or throw him over the wall? Something. Anything. He didn't think he had the capacity to take on this story. He didn't want to know another thing. If it wasn't for Dante, the ultimate wild card in this ridiculous game, he'd have stood up and walked away, wanting no part of yet another person's pain.

He forced himself to speak. "So isn't that even more reason *not* to leave Dante? No matter what?"

"My daughter is alive, Newt. Do you hear me?

75

She's with my brother, and up until a few hours ago I thought they'd both been dead for weeks. I don't even like saying it out loud, just in case the universe is as whacked as I think it is and somehow I'm jinxing the whole thing, devil laughing his ass off, God himself giggling up above. Lord have mercy, amen, hallelujah."

"Keisha?"

She looked at him, tears brimming her eyes. "What."

"You're saying some weird stuff. How's your mind?"

"My mind is a big pile of crap, Newt. But I have to get out of this place and go get my daughter. There are no other options under the heavens. Hear me? None. It should only take a day, probably less. Even if Dante was all by himself, he could survive that. It's worth the risk so that I can bring my daughter back here and we can... live out our days."

He didn't understand—much less agree—with her plan. He didn't fully believe she was of sound mind, talking sense. And no matter what lay behind this giant story, which had only been cracked, he could not bring himself to support the idea that it had been okay to leave Dante behind. But hadn't Newt's life been a long series of impossible choices? Yes, it had.

"So you're hoping to buy your way out," he said, "go find your brother, who has your daughter, then bring her back here? You think she'll have a better life here than with your brother?"

It was the wrong thing to say. The pain that came over her face almost physically hurt him. How could he expect her to be rational in an irrational world, especially one in which she had the bloody Flare and was going crazy, day by day. Maybe hour by hour.

"I'm glad things are so straight-forward for you," she said, the bitterness hard. "But I'll make my own decisions when it comes to *my* children, thank you very much. Now, will you take care of Dante until I get back or not? If not, please take him to Terry and Maria. I'm leaving."

She stood up, holding her son uncertainly. For all her brave words, she obviously didn't know quite how to hand the kid over and abandon him again. Newt hoped he didn't regret his next words, his mind having run a series of thoughts faster then he would've guessed possible based on the last few days.

"I have an idea," he said. "What's your daughter's name?"

She raised her eyebrows, no doubt not in the mood for his harebrained ideas. "Her name is Jackie and she's 10 years old. Now what's going on?"

"Please," he said. "Just sit down and give me one minute. Maybe two. Then if you still wanna go, I swear on my life I'll watch the little guy until you make it back."

It took her a few seconds, maybe holding onto some pride, but she finally did as he asked.

"Okay. A minute and a half, then. Go." She smiled with fake, exaggerated politeness.

He spoke as fast as his mind could keep up. "I know this story of yours is a thousand times worse than it even sounds, and it sounds horrible. And I'm sorry. Truly. And I have no right to tell you your business, especially when it comes to your kids. But... it'd be so much better if you could reunite and live with your brother and Jackie out *there* instead of in here. And I need something to live for, especially after seeing the bloody Central Zone—don't ask, I'll tell you later. We all need this. I think I can get us some help, figure things out, and bust our way out of here. A whole group of us. Then we'll get you and Dante back with your family, and take it from there. But getting you to your daughter will be our number one priority. I know it seems like I haven't had time to think this through, but I want to do this. For you. For Dante. For me. For Jackie."

He paused, not sure he'd taken a single breath while rattling all of that out. "I just need a little time to make a plan. What do you think?" He wasn't entirely sure his stream of consciousness had made a lick of sense.

Keisha didn't answer right away. She smoothed a hand over Dante's head, a distant look in her eyes as she considered what Newt had offered. He was, of course, thinking of the man with greasy hair outside the entrance to the Central Zone. Jonesy. He'd almost seemed fanatical in wanting to protect him. Newt planned to take him up on it. He waited for Keisha to respond. She finally did.

"Why would you want to do this for me?" she asked, most of her tough persona gone for the moment. "Aside from the fact that it's not going to be as easy as you say to get out of here, what's in it for you?"

"It can't be any harder than you trying to bribe your way out, then sneak back in with a daughter. Plus, going all by yourself? That whole plan just gives me a sick feeling inside. I doubt Dante would ever see you again."

Keisha sighed. "I said *aside* from all that. What's in it for you?"

Newt stood up and put his backpack on, acting as if she'd already made her decision. "I need something to live for. I need a purpose. I need to accomplish something good before I lose my mind. And I want to help Dante. And you." He meant every word of it, utterly. "And I wanna meet that daughter of yours, see if Jackie's as stubborn as her mum."

Keisha wiped away a tear. "You're a slick son of a gun, aren't you?"

"Whatever that means. Yeah, sure." He held a hand out and she took it, then delicately got to her feet, balancing Dante on one hip.

"Thank you," she said. "I'm in."

Chapter Twelve

The best result of their shenanigans for the day was the large bag of food in their possession, at least half of it edible. And another bag apparently buried in the dirt behind the hut. Newt intended to retrieve his clothes and journal before sunset, but first he wanted something to eat. He and Keisha had been digging through the canvas bag.

Newt held up a can of pre-cooked chili. The label was faded and the expiration date had passed but he didn't care. In the apocalypse, beggars can't be choosers. He wanted chili. He wanted chili bad.

"This," he said. "This is our dinner. Please tell me that as you burgled half the neighborhood, you also burgled a can-opener."

"Didn't need to, smarty pants. I've got one of those fancy pocket knives that can do one-thousand-and-one things. Believe it or not, it even has a knife!"

She cackled at that one, thinking she was pretty damn clever. Newt liked to see it.

"Does your magical pocket knife also have some matches?" he asked. "I'm completely willing to suck down this chili cold, but if we can heat it up, I'll be one happy Newt."

"No, but I have flint and steel. Don't tell me you

don't know how to do that or this whole thing is off. Surely, in this world of ours, you can start a fire without any matches."

"Duh. Of course I can." He couldn't. They'd always had matches in the Glade.

"Good. Let's gather some wood. I'm starving."

* * *

Later that night, after he'd written in his journal and long after the sun went down, Newt lay curled up in the same corner he'd slept the night before—which seemed like a gazillion years ago. All was dark and all was quiet. Mostly quiet. Crickets chirped outside and Keisha was back to her soothing ocean-sound snore. Dante's snore was also soft; Newt could almost believe a little puppy slept on the other side of the room. Weariness pulled at him like a sinking tide.

What had he gotten himself into? He didn't regret what he'd done, what he'd promised Keisha. In fact, he cringed at the thought of *not* having done it. His mind kept going down rabbit holes of alternate endings to the day's events. Chickening out. Keisha saying no. Not getting to Keisha in time, before she attempted bribing her way past the guards. Of course, the day could've gone a hundred disastrous ways— Crank Palace, apocalypse, all that. But they were alive, and they had a goal. He felt good.

But that didn't mean he wasn't bloody nervous. Nervous as hell.

But a good nervous all the same.

When he'd written that curt, heartless note to Thomas and the others inside the Berg, telling them he was going to live with the other Cranks, he'd thought he had a plan. What an idiot. What did Minho always call idiots? Slinthead. That's what Newt was and always would be.

But now he *did* have a plan. His plan even had steps. Find the man with the greasy hair. Jonesy. Tell him what he wanted. Figure out how to do it. Then do it. Simple as that. Save Keisha and Dante and then what happened after that, who cared. If that little family could—

A sharp pain stabbed Newt right behind the eyes. He heaved himself off his back, rocked forward, curled into a ball, grabbed the sides of his head with both hands. The pain didn't stop, kept slicing back and forth inside his skull, as if someone were trying to saw his brain in half. He muffled the cries that wanted to leap from his chest; on some misty level of awareness he didn't want to wake Keisha, didn't want to alarm her. He squeezed his head, rubbed at his temples, prayed to all known gods that it would go away.

The pain lasted a minute at most. Probably more like 30 seconds. But then it faded, quickly descending into a dull ache, and then going away completely. He sat up, pushed his back into the corner, tried to catch his breath without being too loud. Holy hell, that had hurt. The relief from its absence was about as blissful a feeling as he'd ever had. He blew out a heavy huff and closed his eyes, leaned his head against the wall. It had something to do with his memories, the Swipe. The virus had attacked it, maybe.

The episode had been triggered by those thoughts of Keisha and her kids. A mom, a son, a daughter. A mom, a brother, a sister. Newt didn't understand the why's or how's or what's. This is what he knew—he'd been stabbed with pain, and then the pain had vanished. And now...

Mom. Dad. Sister.

Newt remembered a little more.

Just enough to make him sad. Just enough to confirm that he needed something to keep him occupied or he would sink forever into the darkness. Sink and never see the light again. Yes. He had to keep occupied. Had to keep busy and leave a last tiny mark on the world.

Which is exactly what he planned to do.

Tomorrow, he'd talk to that Jonesy guy.

Part 2
Light at the End of the Freeway

Chapter Thirteen

The bowling alley was hot.

And it stank. It stank to high heaven—something his mom used to say. Usually in regards to his bedroom. No matter how much he pushed his dirty clothes and socks into the deepest reaches of the closet, the stench always wafted out when his mom walked into that room. He'd then say she attracted such things like moth to a flame, like fingers to a booger, just to make his sister laugh.

He laughed right then, in the present day, no sister in sight, a nice belt of a chortle that made everyone within 20 feet give him a wary look. That made him laugh even harder. Jonesy, his new bodyguard, greasy hair still greasy, gave him a courtesy chuckle of his own, though he couldn't possibly know what had set Newt off.

A few days had passed since Newt's headache. Since Keisha had agreed to his plan. Since a few memories of his family had come back to haunt him, as much of it written in his journal as possible. He kept the thing with him at all times, tucked into various pockets, some homemade.

But Newt was starting to... slip.

To slip into an abyss.

The abyss.

He couldn't deny it anymore. His mind... jittered, now. It quaked. The bloody thing had the bloody palsy. Keeping his thoughts still amongst all that squishy commotion had become tougher with every passing hour of every passing day. His hold on reality was loosening, in both the here and now and in that beautiful, painful, remembered past, loosening with each hour that ticked on by with no remorse.

But for the moment, he only had one thing to hold onto. And that was enough.

He sat on the far left lane of the old alley, where the crowd was sparse, staring at the fires that roared in the pin caves, a long row of them, like teeth of flames. He had the Launcher cradled in his lap—he'd had to take it back from a guard three times already, each one successively with a little more violence. He thought they'd pretty much leave him alone after what had happened that morning. As Newt had joked when one of the women in the alley saw him all scratched up— "You should've seen the other guys."

He sat. And pondered. Wrote in his journal. Rested. Tried to contain his excitement for the big plan tomorrow.

"Hey, Newt!" He didn't answer. He never answered. People bugged him all the time—"all the time" being a relative term considering he'd only been there a few days—and he'd found that if it was something important they'd actually come up to him. So he kept quiet, mostly. He was the closest thing to famous they had in the Crank Palace.

"Newt, man!" Someone nudged him on the shoulder. He turned around.

Jonesy stood there with two of the Munie

guards—the short fat one and the tall dude with the mustache. All of the guards were on highest alert because of the small riot that morning, and they knew that part of keeping the peace now included playing it cool with Newt and his cronies. Newt liked to think of them as cronies. He'd always wanted cronies.

"What's going on?" Newt asked. Maybe they'd decided to arrest him.

The short guy answered. He was always the first one to open his trap.

"Some people are here to see you," he said. Every word he ever uttered showed just how much he hated his job—like each syllable was a stone to be lifted.

Newt sighed. "Tell them what I tell everyone else. No stories about the Maze, no stories about WICKED, no stories about anything. I'm an un-storyteller."

"I'm not gonna sit here and argue with you, Mr. God-Almighty. They paid me to deliver a message and that's why I did. I don't give a rat's patooty whether you see them or not."

"Paid you?" Jonesy asked. "People are *paying* to see him, now?" There was a hint of regret in his voice, as if their planned escape with Keisha might prevent him a golden business opportunity.

"They came here in a Berg," Tall Mustache said. "They're not your typical lowlife Cranks."

Newt didn't hear the last few words. All he heard was "Berg." After that a roaring sound buzzed in his ears. The bowling alley tilted before his eyes. Nausea swam up his gut, up his throat. He had to swallow back some bile.

He composed himself. "What do you mean they came here in a Berg? What..."

89

He wanted it to be true. He wanted it not to be true.

"Exactly what part of that sentence did you not understand?" Short and Fat said. "Now do you want to see them or not? Yes or no?"

"Did they give you any names?" Newt asked, stalling more than anything. He knew the answer before they were spoken, almost as if he were manipulating the guard's mouth as he answered.

"Thomas... Minho... Brenda, I think. Some other guy who was the pilot."

Newt had spent several days building himself back up, even as he felt his mind slipping. He'd solidified his little security group with Jonesy and his cronies—sounded like a damn rock band in the old world—he'd gotten used to a post-Thomas, post-WICKED life, planned an escape, settled on short-term goals to wrap up his life. That very morning he'd willingly and almost gleefully taken part in a riot, the recipient of only one or two less punches than he'd given. It had felt great, exhilarating, intoxicating. Tomorrow they were going on the last and great adventure of their lifetimes.

And this stupid, petulant, arrogant guard who barely came to Newt's chest had just taken it all away with a few words. Why? Why would Tommy come here? What would it take for him to leave Newt alone, to let him deal with having the Flare in the way he needed? Newt had finally come to terms, finally felt whole. Why couldn't they just leave him alone?

"Hey!" the guard yelled, snapping Newt out of his frustrated line of thoughts. "Yes or no? What's *wrong* with you? You've got three seconds to answer."

Newt couldn't. He simply couldn't. It would break him, shatter him once and for all.

"No," he replied in as firm a voice as he could muster. "Tell them I said to get lost."

"You're su—" Tall Mustache started to say.

"*NO!*" Newt screamed. "Don't let them come near me! Ever!"

Lights swam before his eyes. He expected a retaliation, the butt of a Launcher slammed into his face, or worse. But he had taken them by surprise, preempted any normal response they may have chosen.

Without saying a word, the short guard and his tall, hairy-lipped friend left the bowling alley.

Newt closed his eyes and tried not to see Tommy in the darkness of his mind. Tried not to see Minho. Tried not to see Jorge or Brenda, Teresa or Alby, Gally or Chuck.

He saw them all.

Chapter Fourteen

Newt faced the wall, his back to the departing guards, to the front entrance, to his new posse, to the world. He fumed as silently as possible, aware that the spectacular anger he felt was beyond irrational, but still unable to do anything about it. Every breath hurt his chest, only filled half his lungs. The decision he'd made to leave his friends and the Berg had been almost impossible, unbearable—but the right one. How could they place this burden on him, forcing him to make that same decision again? He shook with rage, cradled the Launcher in his arms like a baby, considered turning it on himself to snap him out of these spiraling thoughts. It wouldn't kill him, after all. But it sure would wake him up.

"Newt, you okay?"

Jonesy. How had Newt chosen to cast his lot with someone like Jonesy instead of relying on his best friends on the planet? He really was losing his mind. *No*, he berated himself. He'd done the only thing he could. Having the Flare was bad enough. Having Tommy and the others around to remind him of just how sad that was... He couldn't take it. He simply couldn't. There was no going back.

"Newt?" Jonesy again.

"I'm fine!" Newt yelled. He turned his head to look at the sallow face of his bodyguard, framed by that ridiculous greasy black hair. "Just leave me alone!"

Jonesy's girlfriend—Newt couldn't remember her name and was pretty sure he never would—lay flat on the ground just a few feet away, groaning after a dose of the Bliss. Newt had never wanted to take the medication so badly as he did in that moment. But his head was muddled enough. He couldn't risk lapsing even further and making a decision he might regret. What could be worse than going back with his friends and then deciding to leave *again*?

He turned back to the wall. Lowered his head. Closed his eyes. Tried to suppress the anger that welled up in him like a surge of acid, like gasoline, lit with a spark, burning and burning. Why had they come back! Why!

Some time passed, his entire body feeling suspended in space, floating in a bubble of hot rage. It might've been an hour. It might've been five minutes, he didn't know. But it took every ounce of his willpower just to keep himself from erupting at anyone within a hundred feet of him. More than once he had to push down the urge to shoot someone else with the Launcher, just to make himself feel better.

"Newt," Jonesy whispered from a few feet away, the harsh kind of breathy whisper that anyone nearby could hear. "The Munie guards brought those people back here! The ones you ran away from!"

Newt's head snapped around. He looked at the front entrance of the bowling alley just as Minho walked into the building, his face shadowed by the outside light behind him. But there was no mistake. And then Tommy entered, right behind him, holding Brenda's hand like a child.

Newt turned back to the wall so quickly that a dizzy spell buzzed his head. He'd caught a glimpse of Jorge right before he'd swiveled.

They'd come for him, anyway. Despite everything. Despite the note he'd written Tommy. Despite the note he'd left in the Berg. Despite the message he'd sent back with that stupid Munie guard. They'd come. A fury came over him that was like a fog of poison gas. On the inside. On the outside, prickling his skin. He shook with it, couldn't stop it. His heart hurt so badly. What was happening to him? Was this what it was like to push past that final barrier of the Flare, into the mad world of the Gone?

"They're almost over here," Jonesy whispered fiercely, panicked for the first time since Newt had met him several days ago. He probably didn't want to lose his new prized possession to its prior owners.

Newt sensed his friends. He heard Minho's breathing, heard the pattern of Tommy's footsteps. He knew these people better than anyone. And for some reason he wanted to yell at them and beat them to a pulp. *I really and truly am slipping*, he thought. *At least I don't have to dread it, anymore.*

It finally spilled out. Newt screamed when he spoke, trying to remember the odd words they'd used in the Glade like a badge of rebellion against their captors. "I told you bloody shanks to get lost!" His pulse took on a life of its own, thumping almost unnaturally in his temples, in his neck, in his wrists, in his chest. He could *hear* it. He swear he could hear it.

Thump, thump, thump. A pounding in his ears, in his brain.

"We need to talk to you."

Minho said this, definitely Minho, though Newt could barely hear him over the rancid drumbeat in his mind. Like someone pumped acid through his heart along with the blood, all of it with a powerful machine, the regular surge of it getting louder within.

Newt sensed a shadow creep over his shoulder. "Don't come any closer." He tried speaking calmly but with vile. "Those thugs brought me here for a reason. They thought I was a bloody Immune holed up in that shuck Berg. Imagine their surprise when they could tell I had the Flare eating my brain. Said they were doing their civic duty when they dumped me in this rat hole." Words rushed out of him in a spasm of lies and deceit, truth no longer mattering. He needed them to leave, at any cost.

Tommy responded, a voice that felt like ice in Newt's ears. "Why do you think we're here, Newt? I'm sorry you had to stay back and got caught. I'm sorry they brought you here. But we can break you out—it doesn't look like..."

The words faded into a roaring static, a buzzing that hurt Newt's skull, all of it kept to the relentless beat of his pulse, which refused to stop, refused to quiet itself to sanity. Newt had the strange sensation that he was deaf, though noise came from everywhere, from inside and out. He felt a panicked loosening of his hold to reality, as if the entire bowling alley were fading from his existence. Movement was all he could do to latch back onto it.

He turned on his butt to face them. He gripped his Launcher like a lifeline.

Minho threw out his hands, said something that Newt couldn't decipher over the roaring in his ears and mind. His old friend took a step back, almost tripping over Jonesy's zonked-out girlfriend. More words, like ants trying to break through the wall of noise.

Newt heard something about the Launcher, asking him where he'd gotten the thing. Newt responded, slurring out a phrase or two, unsure of what he said. Some kind of lie. His hands shook so much he felt the rattle of the weapon through his bones. This obviously wasn't going to work. He forced himself to gain a grasp, to push away the haze of rage. Just a little. Just enough. Anything it took, now. They had to leave. They had to. How much longer could Newt take this?

He pleaded, threw every ounce of his concentration into speaking sincerely but firmly.

Anything it took.

"I'm... not well," he said. "Honestly, I appreciate you buggin' shanks coming for me. I mean it. But this is where it bloody ends. This is when you turn around and walk back out that door and head for your Berg and fly away. Do you understand me?" Every word was an effort. His hands trembled with frustration.

Minho was speaking. "No, Newt, I don't understand. We risked our necks to come to this place and you're our friend and we're taking you home. You wanna whine and cry while you go crazy, that's fine. But you're gonna do it with us, not with these shuck Cranks."

Newt leapt to his feet, feeling a strength in his legs that wasn't there seconds before. Tommy must've seen something crazy in his eyes because he stumbled backward and almost tripped. Newt pointed the Launcher at Minho and unleashed more anger.

"I *am* a Crank, Minho! I *am* a Crank. Why can't you get that through your bloody head? If you had the Flare and knew what you were about to go through, would you want your friends to stand around and watch? Huh? Would you want that?"

He wanted them to argue. Fight him. Give him an excuse. But they only looked back with stunned expressions.

Newt lowered his voice and poured all the venom he could into his next words. "And *you*, Tommy. You've got a lot of nerve coming here and asking me to leave with you. A lot of bloody nerve. The sight of you makes me sick."

Thomas's face melted in sorrow. "What are you talking about?"

Newt suddenly saw himself from above, almost magically. His craziness. He lowered his weapon and looked at the floor. The rage had reached something like an even boil within him.

"Newt, I don't get it," Thomas continued. "Why are you saying all this?"

"I'm sorry, guys. I'm sorry." The apology barely escaped his lips. This was unbearable. All of it. "But I need you to listen to me. I'm getting worse by the hour and I don't have many sane ones left. Please leave."

Thomas started to answer but Newt didn't let him, held up a hand of warning and shouted, "No!" Then he tried again to let the words pour out of him, say anything to appeal to their senses. "No more talking from you. Just... please. Please leave. I'm begging you. I'm begging you to do this one thing for me. As sincerely as I've ever asked for anything in my life, I want you to do this for me. There's a group I've met that are a lot like me and they're planning to break out and head for Denver later today. I'm going with them."

I can help Keisha and Dante, he thought. *I can't help you*. He was able to breathe again, let the anger simmer. He was standing his ground, and that was enough to soothe him. A little.

"I don't expect you to understand," he continued, "but I can't be with you guys anymore. It's gonna be hard enough for me now, and it'll make it worse if I know you have to witness it. Or worst of all, if I hurt you. So let's say our bloody good-byes and then you can promise to remember me from the good old days."

"I can't do that," Minho said. Far too calmly. With far too much confidence.

This set Newt off again. He screamed something that his mind forgot as each phrase came tumbling from his mouth. Trying to still his trembling hands, he held onto the Launcher so tightly his veins popped out. "Get *out* of here!"

The situation was a powder keg. The situation was a disaster.

With one finger, Jonesy poked Thomas from behind, who spun around only to be poked again, this time in the chest. The other members of Newt's gang of Cranks piled up behind Jonesy, like water at a dam.

"I believe our new friend asked you people to leave him alone," Jonesy said.

Thomas didn't back down. "This is none of your business. He was our friend way before he came here."

Jonesy slicked back his hair, the virus having turned him into a storybook villain. "That boy's a Crank now, and so are we. That makes him our business. Now *leave* him... *alone*."

It was Minho's turn. "Hey, psycho, maybe your ears are clogged with the Flare. This is between us and Newt. *You* leave."

The powder keg sprung a leak; a match ignited and grew closer.

Jonesy raised a hand, a shard of glass squeezed tightly in his grasp, enough to make him bleed. "I was hoping you would resist. I've been bored."

The powder keg met the flame.

Jonesy the fool lashed out with his weapon, tried to gash Tommy across the face. The world tilted right before Newt's eyes, but it was only Thomas falling to the ground to avoid the sharp piece of glass. But Brenda had stepped up, knocked Jonesy's arm with a hard chop; the glass flew out of the man's hand and shattered against the wall. Then Minho barged in, tackled Jonesy; they both crashed to the floor, right on top of the drugged-out girlfriend. Bliss or no Bliss, she screamed a gurgling scream, kicked and flailed at anything that would move. Enough punches landed to begin a brawl; Newt couldn't tell whose arms and legs were whose.

Then his vision clouded, a white fog pouring into his eyes, and the storm of noise returned. The buzzing. The roar. The *thump, thump, thump* of his impossible pulse. He screamed, although it seemed to be within a long tunnel, forever echoing.

"Stop it! Stop it now! Stop or I'll—" He didn't know how he finished the thought. He had lost control of himself, distantly felt the Launcher in his hands, sweeping back and forth as if he sprayed the bullets of a machine gun. He shook with unspeakable rage, losing his mind to it. Not knowing what else to do, how else to expend the incredible energy building inside of him, he pulled the trigger.

Through the cloud of white he barely saw the Launcher grenade strike Jonesy and explode in blue flashes. Newt heard nothing but his own noise. Tendrils of lightning danced across Jonesy's body as he collapsed, writhed, drooled.

Newt held it together by a spider's thread, hoping it would be over soon. Whispering, he said, "I told him to stop. Now you guys leave. No more discussion. I'm sorry."

Minho tried to say something but all Newt heard was noise on top of noise.

"Go." Newt strained to speak. "I asked nicely. Now I'm telling. This is hard enough. Go."

Minho said something about all of them going outside to talk. Newt pulled up his Launcher into firing position, stumbled a step or two toward his old friend.

"Go! Get out of here!"

Thomas and Minho spoke to each other. Newt heard nothing, but more words leaked out of his own mouth. "I'm sorry. I'm... I'm going to shoot if you don't go. Now."

They turned to leave, unspeakable pain on their faces.

They were leaving him.

He wanted them to.

He hated them for doing it.

Tommy. Minho. Brenda. Jorge. Walking away. Out the door.

Newt fell to one knee, knowing he couldn't have lasted another minute. He spoke aloud to anyone who might listen.

"Chase them. Make sure they don't come back."

He collapsed to the ground and tears poured from his fogged eyes, though it had nothing to do with madness.

Chapter Fifteen

It took three hours for Newt's heart to settle back to a normal beat, for the blur of his vision to crystallize into clarity, for the roar in his ears to fade away to quiet. Somehow he'd made it back to his little shack though he remembered nothing of how he got there. He slept, though he didn't remember falling asleep or waking up. He'd closed his eyes and opened them again a thousand times, willing that white haze to depart from his vision. The noise dissipated too slowly to notice, and then seemed gone in an instant.

But his head still hurt. He imagined it would hurt more often than not from then on.

"Newt?"

He looked up from a spot on the floor, saw Keisha, her eyes filled with concern. She'd probably been with him for a while, but as far as he could remember, this was the first time he'd seen her since the riots ended that morning.

"You feeling like yourself again?" she asked. Dante appeared then, Keisha dangling the kid in front of Newt's face to cheer him up. "You wanna try to sit up?"

Newt tried to nod, failed. Tried to speak, but only got out a grunt. So he got his hands under him and pushed his body up and around to sit with his back against the wall. The world swam for a minute but then settled back into position. Surprisingly, the movement didn't send a shockwave of pain through his skull. He was better. He was definitely better.

Keisha and he exchanged a long look, their eyes showing sadness for the day past and fear for the next one up.

"Wanna talk or... nah?" She finally asked. "Maybe we should postpone—"

"No!" Newt snapped, grimacing at the pinch of pain in his forehead. "No way. There's no way in hell we're bloody postponing anything. We're getting you to your family. Tomorrow. I need that more than you do."

Keisha nodded and kept nodding, as if she wanted to say something but had to fight back tears. After a hundred times or so, she'd finally stopped asking him if he was sure about trying to bust out and find her family. But it obviously still touched her and frightened her, both. It scared him, too, but for some reason it was now the sole purpose of his life, the only thing that prevented his mind from slipping into that ever-expanding void of... dissonance.

"Tell me about today," Keisha said quietly. "How bad was it? That walking freak Jonesy... he wouldn't know an intelligent conversation if it leaped up and bit him on the nose. I barely understood 10 words when he dropped you off."

"Jonesy brought me back?" Newt asked. "I shot him with a bloody Launcher grenade!"

"Yeah. He said to tell you that he forgives you and that he knows you did it by accident. He actually laughed about it. Dude's hilarious."

Newt made a sound that slightly resembled a laugh. "Can I have some water—I feel like I swallowed a bucket of dirt." He didn't mention that he wasn't so sure it *had* been an accident when he shot Jonesy. He certainly deserved it for attacking Tommy. Oh well. The guy was merely a tool, anyway.

They had an old milk jug full of clean water and Keisha poured him a cup. When she handed it to him, she repeated, "How bad was it?"

He drank the water in one long series of gulps, gasping for air when he finished. "It was bad," he finally said. "I guess I know what it's gonna be like, now, when we push past the Gone. I went bonkers, Keisha. Completely bonkers. I couldn't see, couldn't hear, couldn't think straight. It's a wonder everyone walked out of that place alive. Especially me."

"Oh, man, Newt. I'm sorry. Something ain't right up there, that's for sure." She tapped her right temple.

"I'm sure the stress had something to do with it," Newt said. "All that ruckus this morning, those idiots attacking the guards for no reason whatsoever. Like that wasn't bad enough—I was exhausted, scratched, bruised. I went to the bowling alley because it was close, thought I'd rest up then come back here. Then, of all the bloody things to happen, my..."

He didn't know what she knew. Even if she *had* understood every word Jonesy said earlier, which she obviously didn't, would it have even mattered? No one fully realized, not even remotely, what Newt had been through inside that old rickety building. The shock of his friends returning, the pain it took to stick to his guns and insist they leave, the trauma of how horrifically it all ended. The despair on Thomas and Minho's face had somehow burned into Newt's mind despite the fact that he'd temporarily lost it.

"Newt?" Keisha prodded. "Tell me what happened in the bowling alley."

"Do I have to?"

"Yes, you do." She smiled, and it made him think of his own mum, returning from the fog of his memories. "Talk to me, boy. It'll make you feel better. I think they used to call it therapy, back before the world went to hell in a hand basket."

"I went crazy," he said, barely above a whisper. "That's all there is to it. I went crazy when I saw Tommy and Minho. He... they were... it's way too long of a story to tell. You've heard some of it. But they were everything to me. *Are* everything to me. It ripped my heart out to get the Flare, to know they were immune and I wasn't. And then it ripped my heart out again—"

"You have two hearts?"

Newt laughed, the kind that popped through your nose. "What is this, comedy-hour now? I'm trying to tell you how bloody miserable I am."

"Ok I'll shut up. Keep going."

He rolled his eyes and shook his head. "Anyway. It just about killed me to leave them after they went into Denver. Yeah, if I'd had two bloody hearts they'd have both been ripped out. So I guess I have three since one's still beating. But... when I heard that they'd come looking for me, and then even worse when they walked into that bowling alley... my mind just started shutting down. I was so mad, so bloody angry, it was like every liquid part of me had started to boil and shoot out steam. I couldn't see, I couldn't hear, I couldn't think. I lost control." He paused, wishing he could describe it better. "Like I said. I went crazy."

"Ugh. I'm so sorry. What happened next?"

Newt shifted his position to give some of the bumps and bruises a break. "I hardly remember any specifics. I was screaming and yelling, Jonesy tried to act like king of the world, people were brawling on the floor. And my mind just wasn't working. I knew I needed my friends to leave. They have something they're trying to accomplish and it's much, much bigger than me. Plus, this is all crappy enough for me without constantly worrying about how hard it would be on *them*."

He shrugged. "So, ya know, I did what any rational human being would do. I waved the Launcher around like a cracked-up junkie, shot Jonesy, started threatening to shoot Minho and anyone else who dared piss me off. Then a bunch of my new Crank buddies chased them out of town and back to their Berg. It all went exactly as I'd planned."

Keisha raised her eyebrows. "Now who's performing comedy-hour?"

"At least I'm funnier than you."

She scoffed. "No offense, Newt, but you have all the humor of my big toe."

Dante made a noise then—the kid was so quiet that it was easy to forget he existed sometimes. He'd been napping in the corner. Keisha scooted over and picked him up, placed him in her lap. Then she hugged him long and hard, maybe imagining her son going through the awful types of things Newt had just described.

"Do you ever regret it?" he asked, pretty sure it was a dumb thing to say.

"Regret what?"

"Bringing kids into this horrible world."

Her look confirmed it. It had been a very dumb thing to say.

"Don't you ever ask a mom that question, Newt. Do you understand what I'm saying to you? Crazy or not, don't ever ask that question."

"I'm sorry. I wish I could take this whole day back."

They sat in silence for a while. Newt decided it would only make matters worse if he kept apologizing. He'd meant it as a way of saying how sorry he felt for Dante, for his future, for the angst she must feel every minute of every hour wondering what lay in that future. And Jackie's.

"You'll be with your daughter soon," he said into the silence. "You and Dante both, along with your brother. You'll be together, and that's something. Maybe you guys have a big purpose in the grand scheme of things. In the universe."

She gave him a look. "Okay, Socrates. Then why didn't you want to be with your friends, huh?"

That stung, more than he was willing to accept. "I told you why. They're trying to accomplish something bigger than—"

Someone banged on the door, hard and fast, then opened it without waiting to be invited. Newt's nerves jumped in alarm but then he saw that it was Jonesy. Then they jumped again because he remembered that he'd shot the poor guy with a Launcher grenade.

"What... a... day!" the man shouted. "What a damn day!"

Newt and Keisha just stared at him, wondering if he had a point.

He finally explained. "All the Munies who worked here up and quit. Just like that. Got together, must've talked all of five minutes, then decided. Opened a gate, took their weapons, walked out. Didn't even bother locking the door. I guess our little riot this morning and the visit from your psycho friends woke them up to just how lame it is to work in the Crank Palace." Then he laughed. He laughed as if he were the happiest man on Earth, his greasy hair shaking with each new chortle.

"You're serious?" Keisha asked. "You mean we don't have to break out?"

He touched his nose and said, "On the button, my good lady."

Keisha looked at Newt. "I think this damn fool has lost his mind."

"Come see for yourself!" Jonesy hollered. "The gate is wide open and people are streaming out like it's a holiday."

He ran off before anyone could respond, probably to share what he thought was good news. Newt wasn't so sure about that.

"What do you think?" he asked Keisha, who looked the opposite of enthused.

She thought a moment before responding.

"What do I think? I think it's a bad sign when the people *with* weapons start running away from the ones who don't."

Chapter Sixteen

Dawn seemed to come late the next day, as if the sun had decided to sleep in, the sky wrapped in gray clouds, the threat of rain heavy and imminent.

They'd decided to get a good night's rest—or what passed for such a thing in the circumstances—before heading out the next day. For one thing, they wanted to maximize their daylight. For another, they didn't want to be wandering the streets with the other escapees in the middle of the night. Talk about spooky. Most of them had already left, and Newt figured they might as well give them a head start, give them some space. The more the better.

They stood outside the little hut they'd called home for a few days. He looked at the pathetic little structure, wondering if he could've spent the rest of his descending days in such a place—with a kid who didn't talk and a woman who only made him miss the shadow of a mother he *almost* remembered. Keisha and Dante already meant the world to him, but staying in this place until they went completely insane sounded like a special kind of hell on Earth.

"Here they come," Keisha said. She had her backpack hitched up, packed to bursting with food and supplies, just like the one on his own back. Dante sat on the ground at her feet, staring at the approaching group of ragamuffins as if to say, "You're putting our lives in the hands of *them*?"

Jonesy lead the group of eight shady-looking Cranks down the path, right on time, one hour past sunrise. Newt didn't know why the word *ragamuffin* had popped into his head just now—surely a term his mum or dad used to describe the teenage hoodlums in the neighborhood—but it seemed to fit. There were more tattoos, piercings, leather boots, and ripped, shoddy clothing than Newt had ever seen in one place. And they apparently weren't too keen on baths or getting haircuts. But they had volunteered to risk their lives to help him reunite Keisha with her family. That said all that needed to be said.

"Master Newt!" Jonesy called out, a huge grin revealing the less-than-full-load of teeth inside his mouth. He slicked his hair back with one hand, a favorite hobby of his. "Are we ready for the adventure of a lifetime?"

Newt gave him a nod, like he'd imagine a cowboy doing in the stories of old. "Actually, hoping for the lamest adventure of my lifetime. With the guards gone, let's hope we can walk straight there and be done with it. Keisha says it's about 20 miles."

Jonesy usually had a goofy, blank look on his face, but he had a flash of something very serious cross him upon hearing Newt's opening salvo. As if he knew, absolutely knew, that there was zero chance on God's green Earth that they'd just stroll to Keisha's meeting place without incident. Without an incident that left scars.

"I hope you're right," Jonesy said, mostly recovering his former, and normal, carefree expression.

"I'm sure you're right. Who'd mess with a bunch of dudes and ladies like us?" He gestured at his friends as if revealing a prized possession. And maybe he was.

Newt noticed, with a sadness that pierced him more strongly than he would've thought, that Jonesy's girlfriend had not come along. He almost asked about her but thought better of it.

"I don't guess the Munies left any Launchers behind?" Keisha asked. "That would've been downright peachy of them if they did."

"Not a one, the bastards," Jonesy replied. "But we've got plenty of sharp objects." He lifted his shirt to reveal a shard of glass tucked into his pants, half of which had been wrapped with black tape. "I'll try not to cut my hand this time."

Keisha eyed him up and down. "Better be careful or you might cut something worse. I wouldn't run too fast with that thing stuck in your pants."

This earned a respectable enough laugh from the group.

"I'll be super duper careful," Jonesy responded. "Shall we get a move on? Sun only stays up for so long, ya know."

"Good that," Newt said, something he hadn't uttered in decades, or so it felt. "Let's get the hell out of this place."

"Who wants to carry the kid first?" Keisha asked.

* * *

Newt refused to believe that each and every guard had left—at least he wouldn't until they'd put the wall a few miles behind them. All the same, he'd taken his

Launcher out of his backpack and held it, charged and ready to "Jones" anyone who needed it—that's what Jonesy kept saying Newt had done to him, like it was a badge of honor. "Remember that time you Jonesed me?" he'd ask. "Oh yeah that was yesterday." Or, "I was Jonesed by a Maze-kid, ain't that a thing?" Newt was really starting to like this guy he'd violently electrocuted not 24 hours ago.

As they approached the gate through which they'd just entered less than a week prior, he saw that it was open, which was a good start. One of the doors had been knocked off a hinge, the big slab tilting toward them. There wasn't a single person in sight.

"Careful, now," Jonesy called out. "Everyone wrap around Newt and his mom, his brother. Keep them in the middle."

"They're not..." He left it. "I'm the one with the Launcher!"

"Don't matter. Do as you're told."

He gave Newt a creepy wink that did nothing to make him think this man was sane enough to be their leader. *Gotta work with what you got*, Newt thought.

They made it to the gate, looking in all directions between the 10 of them—11 if you counted Dante, but he wasn't much good as a lookout. Newt eyed the doors, expecting the boogeyman to jump out at any moment. The gray morning made it hard to adjust his eyes between the lights and the darks. But the world seemed abandoned by the human race. The sounds of birds were the only signs of life besides his little group.

They passed under the archway created by the open gate. No one jumped from the top of the wall; no one sprinted out of the woods; no one swooped down

114

from the sky with man-made wings. They were alone, at least for the time being.

Newt looked back up at the wall, remembering that he'd seen a sign on the way in but didn't catch the words in time as their truck zoomed past. It was just a piece of wood that someone had nailed to the planks of the main structure, a short message scratched onto its surface with a nail. Then someone had filled in the grooves of the words with dark mud, now dried.

HERE THERE BE CRANKS, it said.

Stupid, Newt thought. Although it struck him that he really was a Crank, now, a word that had become synonymous with monstrous ghoulish cannibal people before he caught the Flare, himself. He knew he'd be there before too long. Soon, if the incident in the bowling alley had been any kind of indicator. Past the Gone. He shuddered as he stared at the sign. He'd wanted Tommy to kill him so he didn't have to go through it all. But Thomas had failed him, hadn't he? Or maybe he hadn't read the note in the envelope, yet. Maybe.

"Hey, Captain Newt," Jonesy said, interrupting his morbid thoughts. "You having another episode or what?"

Newt turned to him. "No, just gonna miss the place, is all. Shame to leave so soon."

He set off after the others, ignoring the urge to look back one last time. And so it was that his short stay at the Crank Palace came to an end, he thought with a melodramatic flair. He swore he'd never come back.

Not alive, anyway.

115

Chapter Seventeen

Twenty miles is a long way to walk, Newt kept thinking, especially when you don't have any sense of how far you've gone or how fast you're moving. But then he imagined what Minho, the oldest veteran of running the Maze, would say if he heard Newt's thoughts. It would probably include the word slinthead, among other less savory things, followed by a condescending laugh, all of which would somehow still fail to hurt his feelings. Tommy would probably just agree with Newt, but then go out and get it done, anyway, without a single complaint.

He missed those guys. He really missed those guys.

The sky remained gray as they traveled, mostly in silence, all 10 of them taking turns with Dante in their arms—although Keisha always stayed close with eyes glued on the kid. Rain had yet to fall despite looking like it would dump on them any second. Newt was thankful for the cooler air, feeling as if his backpack weighed a thousand pounds. They made their way down small village streets and long country roads, not yet to the suburbs, where things might get more dicey. So far they hadn't seen anyone out in the open.

The wind blew as they walked, at their backs, pushing them along. Every bit helped.

"Maybe you should check it again," Newt whispered to Keisha in one of the few times that Jonesy let them separate from the group a little. The others were 30 or 40 feet ahead of their pace. "We can't afford to waste time." It was his turn to hold Dante, who slept on Newt's shoulder, snoring softly and sweating like it was the Scorch itself they walked through.

She side-eyed him, having the same problem he did. As soon as they talked about their one big secret, the cell phone, they just assumed that the others were super-spies who had super-hearing and super-vision. And the both of them were terrible at keeping it cool under those circumstances. In reality, having a functioning cell phone should be so bonkers that no one could possibly suspect. But they'd both agreed that letting Jonesy and his goons know about the magical device would be a monumentally bad idea. Saints, they were not, no matter their constant bowing and scraping to the Almighty Newt or whatever moniker Jonesy last chose for him.

"I know where to go, Newt," Keisha said so quietly he barely heard her. "I've lived here my whole life and so has my brother. I'm not an idiot."

"That's not what I meant." He carefully shifted Dante to his other shoulder, wishing the boy would just wake up and relieve him of the pain in his back—what a great brother Newt had turned out to be. Uncle? Whatever. "Would you really be surprised if something came up and he had to change the plans? Change the meeting place? What if we get there and don't find them and waste all this time? Just check it."

Keisha sighed heavily, not hiding her displeasure.

"I'm scared to, okay? It traumatizes me every time I turn that stupid thing on. I just know it's going to have horrific news. Not to mention that the battery is really getting low. Almost out."

"I get it," he said, though he wasn't sure he did. Surely it was worth it to check really quickly, keep it on for just a few seconds. He didn't bother saying that, however, because he wasn't in the mood for another lecture about how powering it on and off used up tons of battery life all on its own. "I would just feel better if we knew the plan is still the plan. You haven't looked since last night before going to sleep."

"You're like an old man with hemorrhoids, you know that? Grumpy all the time, worried all the time, face lookin' like you're constipated. It's a wonder Dante isn't terrified of you."

Her smile offset every word she said.

Newt patted Dante on the back. "This kid loves me and you know it. Probably more than he loves you. He even told me that this morning."

"He doesn't talk."

"Oh, yeah." They walked for a minute or two, her silence driving him crazy. "So you're really not going to check? Real quick?"

Another heavy sigh blew through her nose and mouth both. "Will it shut you up if I do?"

"I swear it."

"Fine. Tell them I'm going to pee."

* * *

When Newt yelled ahead for the others to stop, Dante woke up, startled by the loud shout.

119

"Sorry, sorry," Newt whispered, trying to imitate the bouncy thing that Keisha did to soothe the kid or get him to fall asleep. "I think my turn's up with you, kid. How did you gain 50 pounds overnight?"

He didn't respond. He never did. But he didn't cry, either, so Newt considered it a victory.

A few minutes later, Keisha came out of the field of tall grass into which she'd disappeared to check her phone and take care of personal business. She waved up at Jonesy, thanked him for taking a break, then walked over to Newt.

"Want me to take him?" she asked.

"Yes. Please." He gladly handed him over. "Well?"

Their glass-shard-armed escorts had started moving again, Jonesy yelling some smart comment about Keisha having a small bladder. Newt and Keisha followed, like stray cattle behind the herd, trying to catch up.

"Was there a message?" Newt asked again, impatience making his head hurt.

Keisha nodded, and the false smile she'd put on for Jonesy disappeared. Newt's heart stopped beating, refused to start again until she told him the news.

"Is it bad?"

"No, no, not necessarily. It just worries me."

"Why? What did it say?"

She gave him a look, her eyes filled with anxiety. "Just one word. *Hurry.*"

* * *

They had about three hours until sunset.

They'd reached the beginnings of the suburbs, a mix of sprawling neighborhoods and small businesses and strip malls. The sight of people had definitely increased, but they usually hid or ran or closed the curtains as soon as they were noticed. So far, Newt had not seen anyone who seemed like a Crank past the Gone.

"I never thought I'd say this," Jonesy said as he scooped something that looked like dog food out of a tin can. "But I'm sick of chili. Especially cold chili."

They were sitting in a circle at the edge of a parking lot, all 11 of them, with Dante playing in the center with a discarded tennis ball they'd found. The establishment looked like it had once been a nail salon and a dry cleaner, two things Newt was sure he'd never see. The windows were boarded up, now, which seemed kind of pointless since both doors had been ripped off their hinges. The rain still threatened heavy up above, trapped in pockets of thick, almost black clouds.

"Did it ever rain in the Maze?" Keisha asked. She was eating a granola bar, and by the looks of it every chew was a solid chore.

Newt took a bite of canned corn to hide his surprise at her mentioning the Maze. Cold canned corn. He hated every kernel but was hungry enough to force it down.

"Yeah, it rained," he said, not comfortable remembering that place. "We had a fake sky, fake sun, fake everything. I don't really know how they made it rain but the place was packed with all kinds of bloody techno gadgets. Stuff that made it seem bigger, more realistic, optical illusions, that kind of crap. I'll never forget the day the sun stopped working. You wanna talk about a freak-out. That was weird."

"How'd it work?" This came from one of

Jonesy's friends, a woman Newt had never heard speak before. "We've heard all kinds of rumors about those places. The experiments. All that scary spooky stuff. I'm sure it was mostly BS."

Newt put his can of corn down, slowly placed the plastic spoon next to it. His hand trembled.

No, no, no, he thought. *No, no, no*. It was happening again. His whole body quaked, whether it was just on the inside or manifested visibly, he didn't know. His stomach turned sour. Pain lanced behind his eyeballs, moving toward the rear of his skull and then forward again, back and forth like a pendulum. He shut his eyes tightly, as if he could squeeze out the pain like juice from a lemon.

Keisha said his name gently. "Newt? Are you okay?"

He nodded but kept his eyes closed. Speaking took an effort and he gasped out the words. "I just have a headache. I don't think I drank enough water or something."

Please, please, please, he thought. *Go away, Flare. Let me get Keisha and this sweet little brat to their family and then take me. Take me fast as you bloody like. I'll be ready for the Gone by then.*

He slowly shook his head. What was he doing, praying to the damn virus?

Someone handed him a bottle of water—he looked up to see Jonesy—the cap already off. He devoured it without taking a single breath. Then he sucked in and blew out air several times to make up for it. Anger, that red mist of fury that had so consumed him in the bowling alley, started to seep through his tissue and bones again. His vision clouded with fog so he closed his eyes again. He had no reason to be angry. None at all.

Go. Away.

Someone lightly touched his shoulder and it was like a claw, a spiked claw with poison tips, surely meant to rip his flesh and make him die of rot and pain. He screamed and swatted it away, opening his eyes to see Keisha. Instead of being mad or scared, she frowned and her eyes filled with sorrow.

"I'm sorry," Newt whispered. "I'm sorry."

She spoke back to him, but he couldn't hear. The roar of white noise filled his ears, kept to the beat of his thumping heart.

"It'll go away," he managed to say. Then he lay on his side and curled into a ball, tightly holding onto his legs, pulled to his chest.

And he waited.

Chapter Eighteen

At some point, mercifully, his mind had decided it was done and fled consciousness, sinking him into a deep sleep. He entered a black void empty of dreams or memories, and it seemed only a few seconds later that Keisha gently awakened him.

She spoke his name several times, and he finally fluttered his eyes open. It was gone. The pain, the noise, the fog. He felt fine.

"Come on, now," Keisha said. "Sit up. It's okay. You're going to be okay."

She grabbed his hands and helped him lift off the hard cement of the parking lot; he swung his legs around and settled into a sitting position. He'd expected a wave of pain or nausea but nothing happened.

"How long was I out?" he asked.

"About an hour. I hated to wake you up but... We're running out of daylight. I knew you wouldn't want us caught out here in the dark. I think we can still make it to the meeting spot on time."

He looked at her, at her kind face. How, in all the big wide world had he stumbled upon someone who could play the role of a big sister? He'd known her for... what? A week? And yet he felt for her some of the same warmth he had begun to feel for his family—

his mom, dad, sister—who were coming out of the misty dark of the memory swipe.

"Thanks, Keisha," he whispered. "You could've dumped me here and kept going. You could've been there by now, even. Thank you."

"Nonsense," she replied with a fake look of reproach. "You promised to get us there, and I don't wanna screw up your pride in your manly abilities. So we decided to wait and let you pretend to save us."

He laughed, a scratchy sound that came up through his throat. "No one's saving anybody. All we're doing is taking a long walk to the family reunion."

"Amen," she said. "Now get your ass up and let's go."

* * *

An hour later, they reached a neighborhood of old homes, most of which were in terrible disrepair—broken windows, shutters hanging by one nail, peeled paint, roofs with only half their tiles. The trees were giant—half of them dead—meaning the place had been there for a very long time. Weeds had replaced lawns a decade or so earlier.

"Perfect place for a grandma house," Jonesy said.

Grandma's. That's where they were meeting Keisha's brother and Jackie. At the entrance to the neighborhood, cracked brick walls still bore signs that said, "Norman Downes." The place sure didn't look as fancy as it sounded, even if it had been brand new.

Keisha hadn't moved since arriving, staring ahead with a blank look. Newt put his arm around her shoulders and gave a squeeze, then pinched Dante on the cheek.

"We made it," he said. "We actually—"

She shushed him hard. "Are you crazy? Don't jinx it." She closed her eyes and bent her neck, putting her chin on the top of Dante's little head. "I'm so scared to walk in there, Newt. Terrified."

He didn't know what to say. He searched for something, anything. "You want me to do it? Tell me which house and I can go check. I'll run."

Instead of answering she handed Dante over, almost pushing him into Newt's chest. Then she slipped her backpack off of her shoulders and lowered it to the ground, bending over it as she unzipped the main pocket.

"Keisha, don't!" he whispered harshly. She had pulled out the cell phone, suddenly not caring that Jonesy and everyone else would see it. "What are you doing?"

"Checking one last time," she said with a dead voice. "Then it won't matter."

"Where'd you get one of those?" a woman in Jonesy's group asked. "I didn't even know those things worked anymore."

Jonesy was the one to answer since Keisha had ignored the question, waiting for the phone to power up. "Only for special people. Uppity-ups and the like. Looks like Newt isn't the only fancy-pants we've been galavantin' with."

The words could've been taken as threatening, but Jonesy had a deflecting look of innocence on his face. More than a few of his pals were whispering to each other, however, and that made Newt nervous.

"Let's just go check," Newt urged. Why was the thing taking so long to wake up? "We're practically there, anyway. Come on."

127

She didn't respond. The glow of the phone finally lit up her face in the fading twilight.

"Lord have mercy," she whispered.

"What?" Newt asked. "What does it say?"

Instead of responding, she started sprinting down the street that lead into the neighborhood, leaving her backpack, her child, and everyone else behind. Newt stood frozen in stunned confusion for a second, then took off after her, Dante held firmly in his arms.

* * *

They passed dozens of houses, dilapidated, roofs falling in, dark as black water on the inside, hovering like another dimension behind broken windows. Keisha turned a corner, then another one. Soon she came to a stop in front of a home that looked in much better shape than its neighbors. There were even lights shining from within, the cough of a generator disrupting the still air of the coming night.

Newt reached Keisha and, gasping for breath, had to put Dante down for a second.

"What did you see on the phone?" he managed to ask.

She looked at him. "It just said, *WICKED is here.*"

"WICKED?" It was so unexpected and his chest hurt so much from sprinting that he felt nothing when he heard the word. "What the hell? Why would they be here?"

"We're about to find out." She picked up Dante and moved toward the front door, which was wide open.

Newt grabbed her arm. "What? No. We... Let's just think for a second."

"They have my daughter, Newt. And my brother. There's nothing to think about." She glared down at his fingers, gripped tightly around her wrist. He let go; his hand flopped to the side as if it had lost its bones. "What's there to lose? Maybe you should leave, though. Seriously. You kinda have a past with them."

Newt shook his head, trying to clear the cobwebs. "I was just a control subject. They shouldn't care about me anymore. Why would it matter? Why are they here?"

Keisha sighed. "That's a lot of questions. I'm going in."

"So am I." When she made to push back, he stopped her. "I've got nothing to lose, either. Not one bloody thing."

"Hard to argue with that one."

She marched across the lawn toward the open door, which stood above three wooden steps and a rickety porch. Newt fell into line right next to her. Up the steps, which creaked with every footfall. She didn't pause at the threshold, walked right in, showing a bravery that reminded Newt of some of the things he'd seen in the Maze. Although terrified out of his wits, he followed her.

They stepped into a wide living room, the kitchen behind it. Two lamps warmly lit the air on either side of a couch that had seen better days, lumpy, torn, collapsed in the middle. In that sunken part sat a man and a pre-teen girl. Behind them, dressed in black and shiny armor similar to the people who'd taken them to the Crank Palace, stood two representatives of WICKED, that fine establishment that had stolen Newt from his parents and treated him like crap ever since. To alleviate any doubt, they wore WICKED insignia on their chests.

"Mom!" the little girl cried, leaping from the couch.

"Jackie," Keisha said almost under her breath; she then rushed forward to meet the girl halfway, pulled her daughter into her arms. The brother then joined them, all four family members squeezing each other in one giant hug. The two guards did nothing to stop the reunion, and they appeared to be staring at Newt through their protective visors.

His heart sank. They were taking him back, weren't they? Of course they were. But why all the fuss over Keisha and her family? They could've taken him at any point. He didn't know what to say so he only looked at the floor, ashamed that he was thinking of himself when this sweet reunion had just happened right in front of his eyes.

After a minute or so, Keisha pulled back a little from her family and looked up at the strangers in their strange gear.

"Why are you in my grandma's house?" she asked them. "What were you planning to do with my daughter and my brother?"

For the first time, one of the unwanted visitors spoke.

"His friends are up to no good, that's why," he said in that filtered, slightly mechanical voice.

The other one pointed at Newt. "We're here for a little collateral." A woman, her voice as hard as the walls of the Maze. "And because the boss said so."

Chapter Nineteen

"What do you mean?" Newt asked. "What's going on with my friends?"

The woman answered. "You know very well what they've been up to. And we might've looked the other way until they started messing with the Right Arm. That's a no-no, Newt. Chancellor Paige has had enough, especially when they pulled the trick with getting their implants taken out. Good thing you still have yours, right?"

Newt didn't need the virus to make the rage boil in his veins. "Why do you people always talk like that? What is so wrong with you that it makes you *enjoy* this stuff?"

"Enjoy?" the woman replied, throwing all the disgust she could into the single word. "You think we like wasting the precious little time we have left in this world dealing with the Munies? Munies who are too selfish to make a few sacrifices to save the whole damn human race?"

It was Newt's turn to repeat her words. "A few sacrifices? Easy for you to say." He didn't know how he said the words so calmly—he wanted to scream them. But no matter what, he couldn't ruin things for Keisha and her family. No matter what.

"Just get on the couch," the man said. "All of you. We're going to record a nice little message for your friends. And don't argue. Please don't argue. I am *not* in the mood."

"What kind of message?" Keisha asked. "What do we have to do with this?"

The man shrugged. "I don't know, lady. Let's just not make this any harder than it has to be, okay? We're just doing our job, and we hate our job. So don't piss us off."

"Okay, but—"

A sharp hollering sound cut her off, coming from the front yard, a mocking, *yoo-hoo* type of catcall. It was followed by another, and then another, this time from the backyard, evident through a broken window in the kitchen. Whoever it was kept it up, shouting and whistling and screaming out things that made no sense, just noise, all of it.

"You gotta be kidding me," the female WICKED guard said. "Are those your Crank friends out there? The ones who came with you from the Palace?"

"I have no idea," Newt said, honestly. He hoped it was Jonesy and the others, but who knew? "What's this video you want us to make? If Tommy and them—"

A booming crash like the end of the world shattered his line of thoughts; he yelled and spun around to see the source of it. A truck—a big beast of a thing with a grill on the front end—had busted through the windows at the front of the house, broken glass and chunks of wood flying in all directions. Even as Newt looked, even as he gaped at the explosive intrusion, a bed plummeted from the ruined ceiling in a rain of plaster, bounced off the top of the truck's cabin, and slid off to the side.

The driver's side door opened and another black-clad WICKED soldier leaned out, most of his body still in the cabin.

"Get in!" he yelled. "There's a whole horde of Cranks out here and more coming!"

Something hit Newt in the middle of his back, sharp and strong. He fell to his knees, looked up at a black visor that reflected a distorted view of his face.

"You have one chance of doing this without being killed," the female guard said. "All of you, in the back seat of the truck, now. Now!" Her companion had run to the passenger side of the vehicle and opened the back door, shooing them toward it like they were his children.

"Just do it," Keisha said, seeming to anticipate Newt going off the wall again. "Just get in the damn truck." She was already ushering her brother and daughter toward the open door. "Sounds like there's a lot more out there than Jonesy and his fool friends, anyway. Come on."

Newt couldn't feel his hands or feet, felt numb all over. He also felt like he couldn't move, kneeling there on the floor like a repentant priest. The guard took care of things for him. She grabbed him by the arm and lifted him with surprising strength, then dragged him to follow Keisha and the others to the truck. Once they were all crammed into the backseat, the soldier slammed the door. She and the other guard quickly got into the front of the cabin. Even before their door was closed, the driver had revved the engine, reversing the vehicle back through all the destruction and debris and into the front yard. The tires spun and all kinds of things crunched, and Newt got a queasy look at faces and arms and hair and wild eyes out in the yard until the truck swerved its way back onto the road. The engines roared as the vehicle barreled down the street toward the exit of the neighborhood.

What in the world just happened? Newt thought to himself. *Couldn't just one thing go right in my life?*

He was scrunched against Keisha, who had both of her children held tightly in her lap. Her brother hadn't made a peep since they'd first arrived; now, he blankly stared out the side window as if he'd given up on life long before this latest turn of events. Keisha didn't say a word; her kids cried as silently as possible. Newt was so enraged he thought every blood vessel in his body might burst from the strain on his nerves, and he didn't think the virus was to blame for much of it. He shook from anger, from all the things WICKED had done to him. It never stopped and it never would.

Three guards in the front, their backs to him, facing forward. Surely there was a way.

The truck slammed on the brakes, throwing Newt forward. His nose crunched against the right headrest, and Keisha and her kids pressed hard against him from the force of the stop. He peeked out the front windshield, saw a line of people in the road, their hands clasped like a thread of paper dolls. Jonesy was in the middle, his eyes lit up with something like ecstasy.

"Why'd you stop!" the female solder yelled.

"Why'd I stop?" the driver yelled back. "Why the hell do you think I stopped? There's people in the road. Are you blind?"

"Well run over them!"

Before he could respond, the front windows on both the driver's and passenger's sides exploded inward with a crack and crash. Arms and hands—it seemed like there were way more than accounted for the number of bodies that could fit in such a space— reached inside, grabbed at the soldiers, pulled on the inner door handles, popped the doors open. The soldiers fought and kicked but all three of them were soon dragged out of the truck, trying to prevent the intruders from ripping off their helmets. The female guard failed and hers came off, revealing a pale white face covered in scars. She screamed as jagged fingernails tore at her to make new ones.

This wasn't just Newt's group from the Crank Palace. There were dozens of people out there, some looking past the Gone, others looking sane but angry. With nightmarish sounds and unbridled energy, they attacked the three WICKED guards with something like primal glee. Clothes were ripped, helmets broken, bodies beat with fists and sticks and rocks found from the side of the road. Newt stared out the window, his disbelief only matched by the rising storm of the Flare in his mind. It was taking over again, triggered by the sights and awful sounds.

"Newt!" Keisha yelled.

He looked at her, barely able to see through the spots that swam before his yes.

"What," he whispered.

"I have my kids and my brother is shell-shocked. Get your ass up there and drive this thing away!"

Shell-shock. Newt didn't know what that was, but he couldn't imagine it would disable a person more than the tide of red rage that swept through his brain and nerves. The roar and buzz of static overtook his hearing again. But he fought through it, held onto whatever he could hold onto. A Crank slipped into the

135

front seat, swinging his legs under the steering wheel, and that's what finally snapped Newt into action.

Roaring like a sprung animal, he heaved himself forward and scrambled over the back of the front bench, reaching for the Crank who'd stolen his way into the truck. Newt grabbed his shoulders, used the man's body as leverage to pull the rest of his own body into the seat. Just as his legs landed in a heap, Newt punched the man in the face, barely connecting since he didn't have his balance yet.

The intruder said nothing, just snarled an inhuman sound that Newt heard as if it came through a wall. Newt got his feet to the floor of the cabin and braced himself, swung another punch at the Crank. The man blocked it, laughing as if he fought off a toddler. He said something, shouting by the looks of the veins popping from his neck, but Newt heard nothing, the words blocked by the crackling buzz in his ears. Something grabbed him from behind; he turned to see a woman had entered from the passenger door, pulling on his shirt. Static electricity frizzled her hair into a furry cloud, framing a filthy face with a huge gash across one cheek.

"Newt!" Keisha yelled, her voice somehow making it through the cacophony of interference caused by his burgeoning madness.

Newt unleashed a buildup of frustration, unsure of what he was even doing. His legs kicked out violently, slamming into the face of the woman, even as he grabbed the man behind the steering wheel and went for his eyes, thumbs poking with all his strength. The Crank swatted at his arms but Newt doubled down, pushing, pushing, kicking again with his legs to add impetus to the effort. He felt his foot connect with flesh behind him, felt his thumb sink through a burst barrier in front. Both Cranks were screaming, clutching at their faces. Newt pushed the man out the driver's door then flopped onto his back to kick at the woman again. He kept at it until she gave up and fell away.

Enraged, on fire, exploding from within, his skin burning, his ears filled with smoldering cotton, his vision blurred by white fog, the air around him seeming to crack like streaks of lightning, Newt fumbled his way upright and sat behind the wheel, put the truck into drive. Then, without worrying about the two open doors, he slammed his foot onto the accelerator.

Tires slipped, then the back of the truck fishtailed. Rubber finally caught on pavement, and the vehicle leaped forward with a burst of speed. They roared away, and Newt was only distantly, peripherally aware of the thumps and bumps of bodies beneath them until they hit clear, open road.

"Jonesy!" Keisha screamed from the back seat. "What about Jonesy!"

Newt heard her, just barely, but he didn't slow the truck. In some other universe he may have felt pity or guilt over leaving Jonesy and the rest of them behind. He even felt a pang thinking that he may have just run his truck over someone who had sworn to help him. But it didn't matter. It didn't matter. The world was Hell, and in Hell things were different.

Keisha, he thought through the clouds of madness that filled his mind.

All that mattered was Keisha.

Dante.

Jackie.

Nothing else.

Chapter Twenty

Newt understood on some level how lucky they were that he was on a relatively straight road, because he was barely holding onto his wits. He forced himself to ease up on the accelerator, felt the force of the engines lessen as the tunnel of vision zooming past his senses slowed, slowed. He looked in the rear view mirror on some instinct, but he couldn't see anything.

"Newt, you can stop!"

Keisha was screaming in his ear, even though it sounded like a whisper.

Newt lifted his foot and pressed down on the brake. The car slammed to a stop, vaulting his body into the steering wheel. Amidst the pulse of his entire body, thumping like a giant heart, he put the car into park. Since the Swipe inflicted by WICKED, he had, of course, never driven. But somehow he had known enough from his prior life, watching his parents drive, memories leaking like water from old pipes, to get them away from the horde of Cranks.

The night settled around them like an ocean of black air, as if they'd sunk to the bottom of an alien sea. As if the sun had been hurled to the other side of the planet. Newt had no memory of sunset, of fading light. And now all was dark and quiet.

"Thattaboy," Keisha said, patting him on the shoulder. The storm inside Newt continued to recede; he could hear her, actually hear her words clearly. Keisha reached up and turned on the little interior truck light, a beacon against the darkness. "I don't know how you just pulled that off back there, but my guess is it's because you've lost your damn mind. Thank goodness."

He looked at her, in disbelief she could say something so cruel. But her face lit up with a smile, a beaming smile, like something from the days before the apocalypse, surely.

"I'm proud of you," she said. "I'm really proud of you."

Newt gave his best attempt at his own smile. Then he closed his eyes and took several deep breaths without saying anything. His nerves calmed, the noise faded, his heart slowed. When he opened his eyes again, no mist obscured his vision. He felt as if someone had lifted a curtain, freeing his mind to see and think freely. And the clearest thought he'd ever had flowed into his mind like clean water from a mountain stream.

He sighed, wondering why his decisions always had to break his heart.

"You have to get out," he said quietly.

"What?" Keisha asked.

"You have to get out of the truck. I need to leave you behind."

Please don't argue, he thought. *Please, please, please. Just understand. Surely you can see what I see.* All of these thoughts went through his mind like a prayer.

"What on Earth are you talking about?" She sounded more hurt than angry.

Newt was ashamed again, this time from the relief that flooded his body after the most recent surge of the Flare's assaulting madness. He turned to face Keisha.

"You can't mess with these people," he said, trying to sort his mind with reason. "Sometimes I think they've given up on finding a cure, and now they're just operating on... I don't know, something like spite. Trying to prove they ever had a reason to exist."

"What does that have to do with anything?" Jackie, who Newt had only heard say one word so far—*Mommy*—squeezed her mother's neck, Dante willing to share for the moment. Keisha hardly seemed to notice, as if her kids were simply appendages of her own body. "I can't tell anymore if you're crazy Newt or regular Newt."

"I'm mostly regular, right now," he said unable to conjure up another smile. "But listen. They'll be coming after us, and there're only two ways they can catch you—find this truck, or track me down. I think we know by now that tracking me down is a bloody cakewalk for them. And they obviously know where their own vehicles are. So..."

He couldn't come out and say it. Surely that had been explanation enough.

Keisha's eyes welled up with tears. "Newt, I'm not having this conversation. We've been to Hell and back together in a very short time and I'm not gonna walk away from you."

Newt tried to squeeze the pain away, hating that she was making this harder than it already was. "Come on, Keisha. Getting you to Jackie was what kept me going. I want my life to end knowing I helped do something good. Maybe you guys can find another car or find a home to settle in. The Flare doesn't seem to be affecting you like it does me. Who knows what'll happen. Maybe you guys will live happily ever after!"

Keisha reached out and twisted his ear. Hard.

He yelped and felt a rush of anger. It took all of his will to tamp it back down.

"I really do have to treat you like a child, don't I?" she said. "Now stop insulting my intelligence. We're all gonna end in misery so we might as well end in misery together. Do you want me to drive?"

"Drive where?" Newt snapped at her. "Where would we go, Keisha? They're gonna track me down and if you're with me then we'll all be wishing for a nice miserable plummet into the Flare. Something terrible is gonna happen, and we both know it. Will you please just take your damn kids and your comatose brother and get out? Let me fend for myself and die without feeling guilty that I brought you with me?"

He was shouting, and he hated himself for it. But they needed to go. They needed to get out of there and let him have this one gift. To know that he was a small part in bringing a family back together before the rage and madness ended what had once been a kid named Newt.

"Please!" he yelled. "Please just get out of the bloody truck!"

"Newt," she whispered, and he saw the fight drain out of her face. She knew. She knew, with a mother's instinct, that he was right. And she gave him another gift—letting him go, something Tommy couldn't do. He could see how much it hurt her, how much it ripped her apart. He had found a second mother, an aunt, a sister...

"Sonya," he said, the word coming out of nowhere. "You remind me of my sister, Sonya. I'm starting to remember her. And she was just like my mom, so I guess you remind me of both. Maybe you're the reason they came back to me." He didn't know why he was saying all this, but it filled him with something very close to joy. "Nothing will make me happier than knowing you guys have a chance to survive out there, together. It'll make up for not knowing what happened to my own family, or if they ever made it. So please go. And do everything in your power to save Dante and Jackie. That's the only thing in the world I want right now. But you have to hurry. I know they're coming. I know it."

Every single part of Newt wanted to break into tears, wanted to bawl his eyes out and sink his face into Keisha's neck, right along with the two kids. But he held it back, just like he'd held back on the ravings of the Flare moments earlier. It wouldn't be long, now, before he'd never be able to do that again. But this would be his last heroic effort. To do what needed to be done for Keisha.

She had no qualms letting the tears flow, and she seemed to struggle for words, her mouth opening and closing several times without speaking.

"It's okay," Newt said. "I know exactly what you're thinking and feeling. You don't have to say anything. All that matters is them." He nodded at the kids. "Jackie and Dante. That's all. And I hope your brother will come around, too." The man stared out the window, crying but quiet, oblivious. *Shell-shocked*, Newt thought. He wondered if the people from WICKED had done something to mess him up so horribly.

Keisha was nodding, wiping her eyes. The inside of

the truck was as silent as a windless plain, and the darkness outside pressed in like something solid and heavy. As if they'd been buried alive, the tiny truck-light like a candle, their last connection to the world above.

"Okay, Newt," Keisha finally said, a strength in her words that made him feel a little better. "I'm gonna let you go. I'm gonna take care of these kids, and help my brother get his wits about him. We're gonna let you go."

"Thank you," Newt replied, feeling stupid but thankful the fight was over.

"But I gotta say one last thing."

Newt nodded, glad for the sheer wisdom and confidence in her eyes. He could leave with that look of hers burned in his mind for the rest of his short life and be happy thinking back on it.

"And here it is," she continued. "Besides my own children, you've done more to lift me up in this world than any other person. I know it was only a few days, but you've..." She took a moment, swallowed. "You've branded me, Newt. You've branded me, and I'll bear your mark forever. God willing, I'll survive this virus and add to what your life meant for this universe of ours. I love you, Newt, and my children will grow up loving you."

He tried to respond, couldn't. But the reluctant tears finally leaked from his eyes. He hoped they said what he didn't know how to put into words.

Keisha took his hand over the seat, kissed it warmly, holding her lips there for several seconds.

"Goodbye, Newt."

It was the only way to end it. She gathered up her children, gently gave a nudge to her brother, and the four of them exited the truck through the door on that side. When it thumped closed, Newt turned back toward the front, put the truck into gear, and drove into the impenetrable darkness.

Chapter Twenty-One

When dawn came, the truck sputtered to a stop. Newt didn't have the slightest clue as to how a truck worked, but the bloody thing had been making weird noises for a couple of hours and when it died, he knew it was dead for good. He'd been driving for a while on a giant, broad road that was filled with scattered vehicles, most of them pushed to the side. The word *freeway* came to his mind, unbidden, and he figured that's what the massive road had been called in the days before the apocalypse.

He sat there, inside a dead truck, for a long time, watching the sunrise over the skyline of Denver. He'd driven aimlessly for most of the night, but when he'd found the freeway he'd decided to head in the direction of the city, marked by just enough light to know it was there. It was a brilliant sight, now, its skyscrapers looking brand new from a distance, framed by growing sunlight, and he longed to travel back in time when such cities ruled the Earth. And you could enter—and leave—as you liked.

Happy. That's how he felt.

He'd lost his backpack and had no food. No possessions except his journal, stuffed in an inside pocket, digging into his leg. The Flare infested his mind, quickly driving him toward the Gone and then past it.

His stolen truck was dead, he had nowhere to go, and no one to talk to. He'd never see Tommy or his other friends again, and he now remembered his family that could very well be dead. He was alone, utterly.

And yet happiness filled his chest. It made no sense, and it was probably just another sign of his encroaching madness, but he gladly accepted it. He'd done something good. Deep down, he had a feeling that Keisha was immune—she'd shown no overt signs of the Flare, at least not around him. And although his part had been tiny, he'd helped her get back to her daughter and her obviously troubled brother. Newt was ending his era of sanity with a positive, hopeful spark. And it made him happy.

He reached into the inseam pocket of his pants and pulled out the journal. Although he should've given the thing to Keisha so that it would hold some future purpose, he was thankful that he could make another few entries. Not quite ready to leave the relative safety of the truck, he opened the small book, unhooked the pen, and began to write.

Maybe someday, somewhere, somehow, the journal would be found and read. And he wanted posterity to know that he had experienced happiness. Not just with Keisha and her family. He had known friends, had shared laughs and adventures with them, felt their love for him and had the joy of returning that love. What else could anyone ask for?

Immunity, food, a big house, a world that wasn't in an apocalypse, a neighborhood filled with all those loved ones? Yeah, that would be better. But still.

I really am going nuts, he thought, and shocked himself with a smile.

Tongue pinched between his lips, he bent over the journal and wrote all these things and more.

Epilogue

Newt had a bullet in his brain.

He didn't understand why he was still alive. He didn't understand much of anything. Vague memories cycled through his diseased mind, and he knew that death was about to come upon him. Whatever essence the world called life, it was quickly draining from him, not in drops, but in torrential cascades through a broken dam.

Tommy had shot him.

Lost in the rage of the Flare, Newt had forced him to do it. He'd begged him to do it. He'd berated him to do it. He knew this only through flashes of images and feelings, almost like it had all been a dream. But the sharp pain in his skull and the fading of the world let him know that it had been all too real. The Flare had ignited in him like never before, an eruption of pure insanity. He'd been almost blind from the white fog, unable to hear over the rush of noise in his ears, the rage so complete that it took complete control, as if some mad tyrant had hijacked his soul.

The details were faint and vanishing from view.

"Newt."

A woman's voice. Softly spoken, directly into his ear. He immediately thought of angels and heaven, wondered if he was about to find out some very good news about the afterlife.

The angel continued. "Newt, I hope you can hear me. I'm sorry to say your vitals are fading and we don't have much time. We tried to save you, I give you my word. We tried with every power at our disposal to save you."

He tried to speak, but it was clear such a thing would never happen again. Why was this woman speaking to him? Who was it? Why had they tried to save him? Despite his life slipping away, he remembered Keisha. Dante. Jackie. He smiled, if only in his ruined mind.

The voice again.

"Newt, listen to me. There are things you need to know. Sonya is your sister, and she's alive. I'll do a better job saving her than I did saving you. I promise."

Newt had a hard time thinking straight. Harder than ever. Thoughts had ceased to form in any coherent manner. But he was aware of the rush of feeling that spread through his heart. Sonya was alive. Sonya was alive. The joy was matched only by his sadness that he'd never see her again, see her with memories intact.

The angel spoke again.

"Newt, I know you think that your life wasn't as important as the rest, that somehow you were a waste because you're not immune." He heard a rumble of frantic voices that had no shape, but it ended with something like a whimper from the woman before she continued. "Oh, Newt, I'm so sorry. Just know this— Sonya is immune and you aren't, and you're siblings, and that's why we had to study you and will keep doing so after..." She cleared her throat, like thunder in his ears. "There has to be some link there, something that will show why the virus affects you but not her. I'll work on that to my last breath."

Newt didn't know if death was like this for all humans, but he felt it as a presence. Though his mind had collapsed into chaos, he saw Life as a light, and Death as something to snuff it out. Even now it was taking in a deep breath, ready to blow with all the might of the universe, ready to blow out the candle that was Newt. The air rushed out of Death's mouth, and Newt felt—and saw—the light weakening, weakening, almost gone.

The angel spoke one last time.

"I have your journal, Newt. If it's my last act on this God-forsaken planet, I'll get it to Thomas. They need to know what you remembered."

Tommy, Newt thought. *Tommy will understand.*

And then the light went out.

About the Author

James Dashner is the *New York Times* bestselling author of the *The Maze Runner* series, which was adapted into a trilogy of movies by 20th Century Fox. He has also written the *Mortality Doctrine* series, the *13th Reality* series, the *Jimmy Fincher Saga*, and two books in *The Infinity Ring* series: *A Mutiny in Time* and *The Iron Empire*.

Dashner was born and raised in Georgia but now lives and writes in the Rocky Mountains.

Other Riverdale Avenue Books
You Might Enjoy

The Macroglint Trilogy by John Patrick Kavanagh
Sixers
Weekend at Prism
Sanctuary Creek

An Outcast State
by Scott D. Smith

Venomoid
by J.A. Kossler

Playing by the Book
by Chris Shirley

Still Hungry For Your Love
Edited by Lori Perkins

The Evoluzion Series by Axl Abbott
Smarter Zombies, Smarter Weapons, Volume One
Redemzion, Volume Two
Stepford Soldiers, Volume Three